THE MIGHTY 12

SUPERHEROES OF GREEK MYTH

BY CHARLES R. SMITH JR. ILLUSTRATED BY P. CRAIG RUSSELL

LITTLE, BROWN AND COMPANY

New York   Boston

I DEDICATE THIS TO ALL YOU COMIC BOOK LOVERS OUT THERE
AND MY MIGHTY THREE: SABINE, ADRIAN AND SEBASTIAN.

LIFE IS LIKE A COMIC BOOK—FULL OF ACTION, SUSPENSE
AND DRAMA—SO ENJOY EVERY PAGE OF IT.

—C.S.

TO SAM, MOLLY, AND JACK.

—P.C.R.

TEXT COPYRIGHT © 2008 BY CHARLES R. SMITH JR.
ILLUSTRATIONS COPYRIGHT © 2008 BY P. CRAIG RUSSELL

COLOR BY LOVERN KINDZIERSKI
BOOK DESIGN BY KIRK BENSHOFF

LITTLE, BROWN AND COMPANY

HACHETTE BOOK GROUP USA
237 PARK AVENUE, NEW YORK, NY 10017
VISIT OUR WEB SITE AT WWW.LB-KIDS.COM

FIRST EDITION: APRIL 2008

ISBN-13: 978-0-316-01043-6
ISBN-10: 0-316-01043-X

10 9 8 7 6 5 4 3 2 1

CPI

PRINTED IN CHINA

THE PRELIMINARY DRAWINGS FOR THIS BOOK WERE DONE IN BLUE AND VIOLET COL-ERASE
PENCIL, FINISHED LINE IN PENCIL USING AN HB LEAD ON STRATHMORE 2PLY PAPER. THE
DRAWINGS WERE COLORED DIGITALLY.

THE TEXT WAS SET IN WILD WORDS, AND THE DISPLAY TYPE IS FUTURA.

CONTENTS

INTRODUCTION—WELCOME TO OLYMPUS ··· 5

ZEUS—GOD OF ALL GODS ··· 9

POSEIDON—GOD OF THE SEA ··· 11

HADES—GOD OF THE UNDERWORLD ··· 12

    CERBERUS—GUARD DOG TO THE UNDERWORLD ··························· 16

HERMES—MESSENGER OF THE GODS ··· 18

APOLLO—GOD OF LIGHT AND MUSIC ··· 23

ARTEMIS—GODDESS OF THE HUNT AND THE MOON ····················· 25

ARES—GOD OF WAR AND STRIFE ··· 29

APHRODITE—GODDESS OF LOVE AND BEAUTY ······················· 30

HEPHAESTUS—GOD OF THE FORGE AND FIRE ······················· 33

ATHENA—GODDESS OF WISDOM ··· 36

    MEDUSA—GORGON ··· 39

HERA—SUPREME GODDESS, GODDESS OF MARRIAGE ·················· 43

DIONYSUS—GOD OF WINE AND REVELRY ································· 45

WHO'S WHO ··· 46

BIBLIOGRAPHY ··· 48

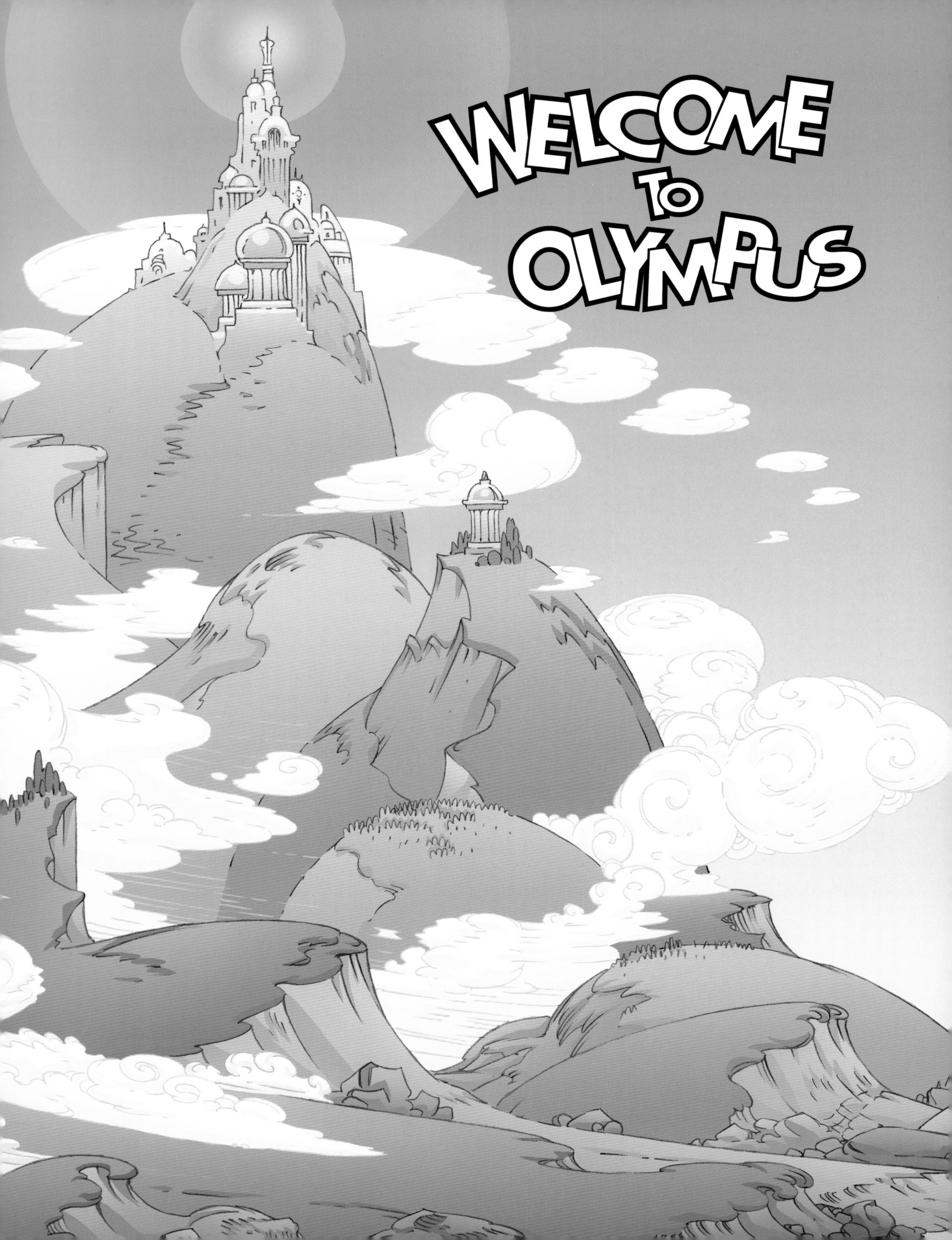
WELCOME
TO
OLYMPUS

WELCOME TO THE WORLD
OF IMMORTAL MEN AND WOMEN,
THE GODS AND GODDESSES OF GREECE
WHO RULE THEIR DOMINION
FROM HIGH ON OLYMPUS,
THEIR ETERNAL HOME,
ABOVE GRECIAN MOUNTAINTOPS
AND CLOUDS WHERE EACH THRONE
SITS
AND SHINES
AND PUTS ON DISPLAY
THE PERSONALITY OF ALL
OLYMPIANS WHILE THEY
WORK
OR PLAY,
CAUSE CHAOS
OR SAY
WICKED WORDS THAT
LEAD MANY ASTRAY.
PLAYING PEOPLE LIKE PAWNS
IN A GRAND GAME OF CHESS
THE GODS OF OLYMPUS
INFINITELY TEST
ASSORTED MORTALS
WHILE TESTING EACH OTHER,
LIKE ***HADES***,
ZEUS,
AND ***POSEIDON***,
TRUE BLOOD BROTHERS
WHO LONG AGO
FOUGHT OVER DOMAINS,
SO THEY DREW STRAWS
TO SEE WHO WOULD CLAIM
THE UNDERWORLD, THE SKY,
AND THE FAR-RANGING SEA,
ZEUS WON THE SKY
AND HIS BROTHERS' ENVY,
BECAUSE NOW HE HAD
THE MOST POWER OF ALL THREE.
SPEAKING OF SIBLINGS,
ARTEMIS AND ***APOLLO***,
THE TWINS, CAN BE FOUND
ON EARTH SLINGING ARROWS
WITHOUT BEING HEARD
AND WITHOUT BEING SEEN,
WHILE ***HERMES*** THE MESSENGER
DARTS IN BETWEEN
OLYMPUS AND
THE UNDERWORLD BELOW,
WHERE CERBERUS THE DOG
GUARDS SOULS AND SHADOWS
AND WELCOMES WARRIORS
FROM THE BATTLEFIELD,
THOSE ENCOURAGED BY ***ARES***
TO SWING SWORD AND SHIELD.
BUT IN BETWEEN WARS
ARES CAN BE
FOUND IN THE ARMS
OF ***APHRODITE***,
THE WIFE OF ***HEPHAESTUS***–
THE SKILLED CRAFTSMAN WHO
DESPITE HIS DEFORMITIES
CRAFTS TRIED AND TRUE
WEAPONS OF WAR
FOR THE LIKES OF ***ATHENA***,
THE WARRIOR GODDESS
WHO CURSED MEDUSA.
MEANWHILE, UP HIGH
WAITING TO SEE
IF HER HUSBAND WILL SHOW
HIS INFIDELITY,
HERA SPIES ZEUS,
LIKE A HAWK EYEING PREY,
WHILE ***DIONYSUS*** DANCES
AND LAUGHS THE DAY AWAY.
EIGHT GODS
FOUR GODDESSES
DO AS THEY DESIRE
WHILE THEIR SISTER HESTIA
TENDS TO THE FIRE
HIGH ON OLYMPUS,
WARMING THEIR HOME,
WAITING TO WELCOME
EACH BACK TO THEIR THRONE.
SO COME ALONG TO MEET
THE GODS OF THE GREEKS
AND WITNESS THE POWERS
AND ADVENTURES OF EACH.

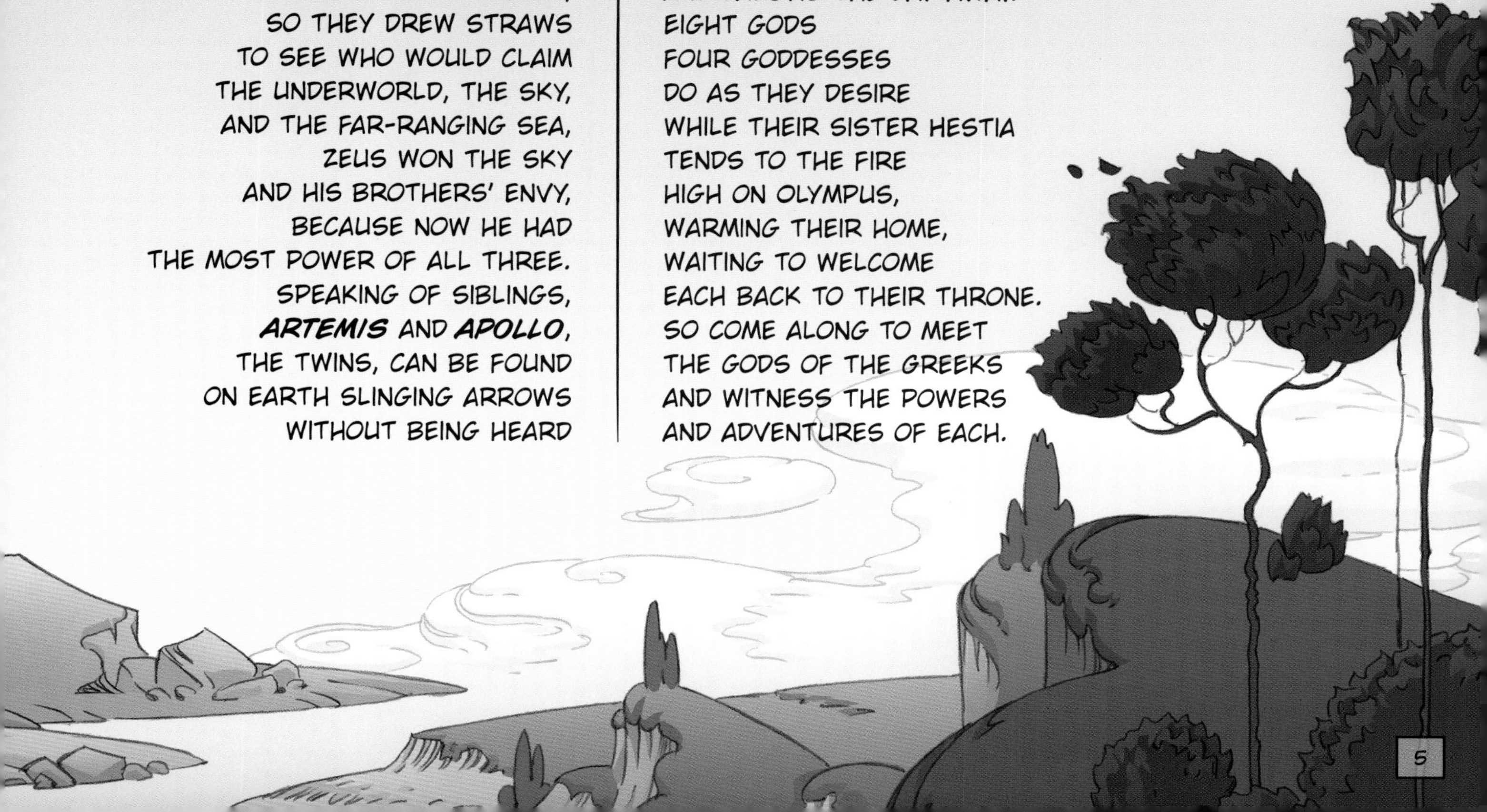

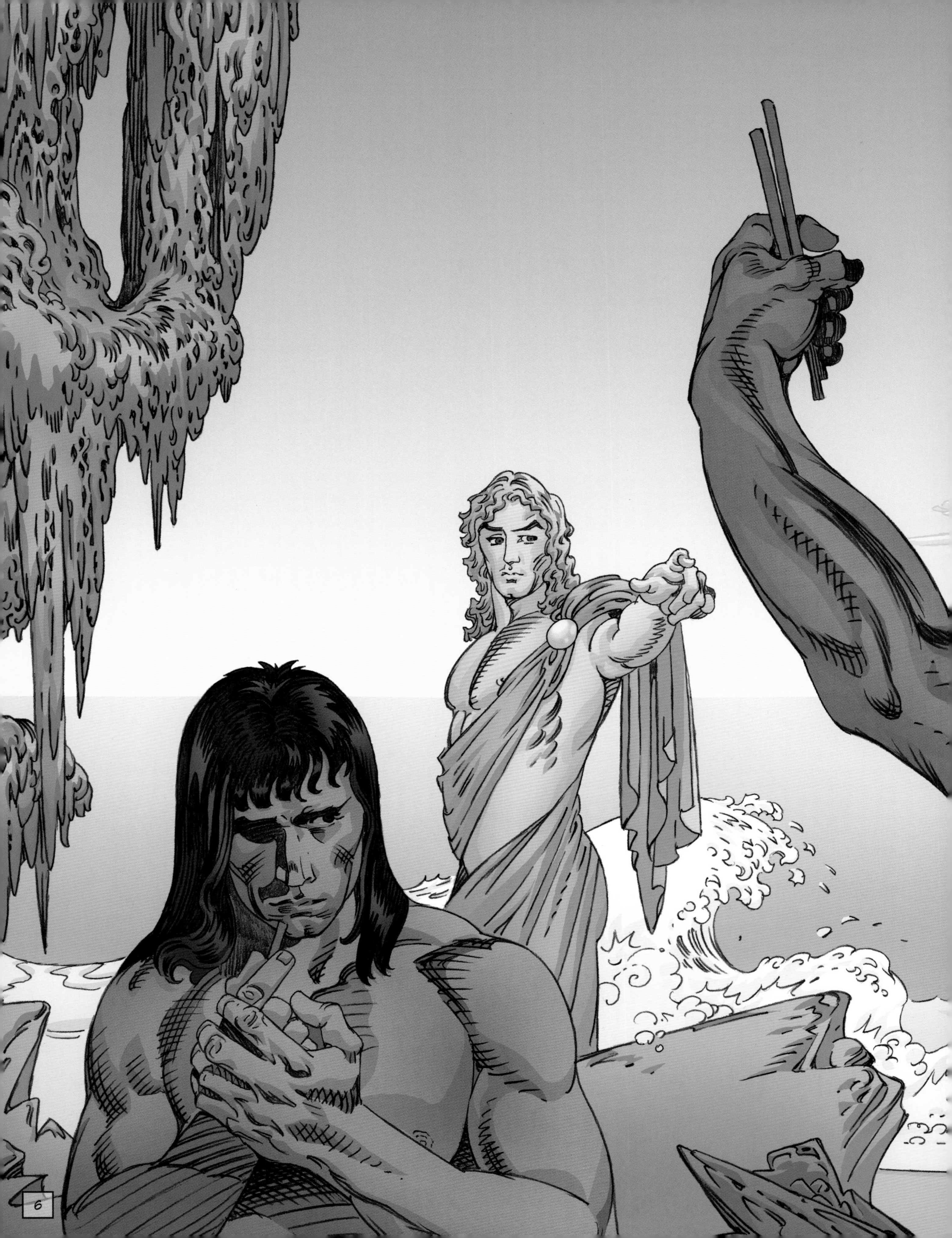

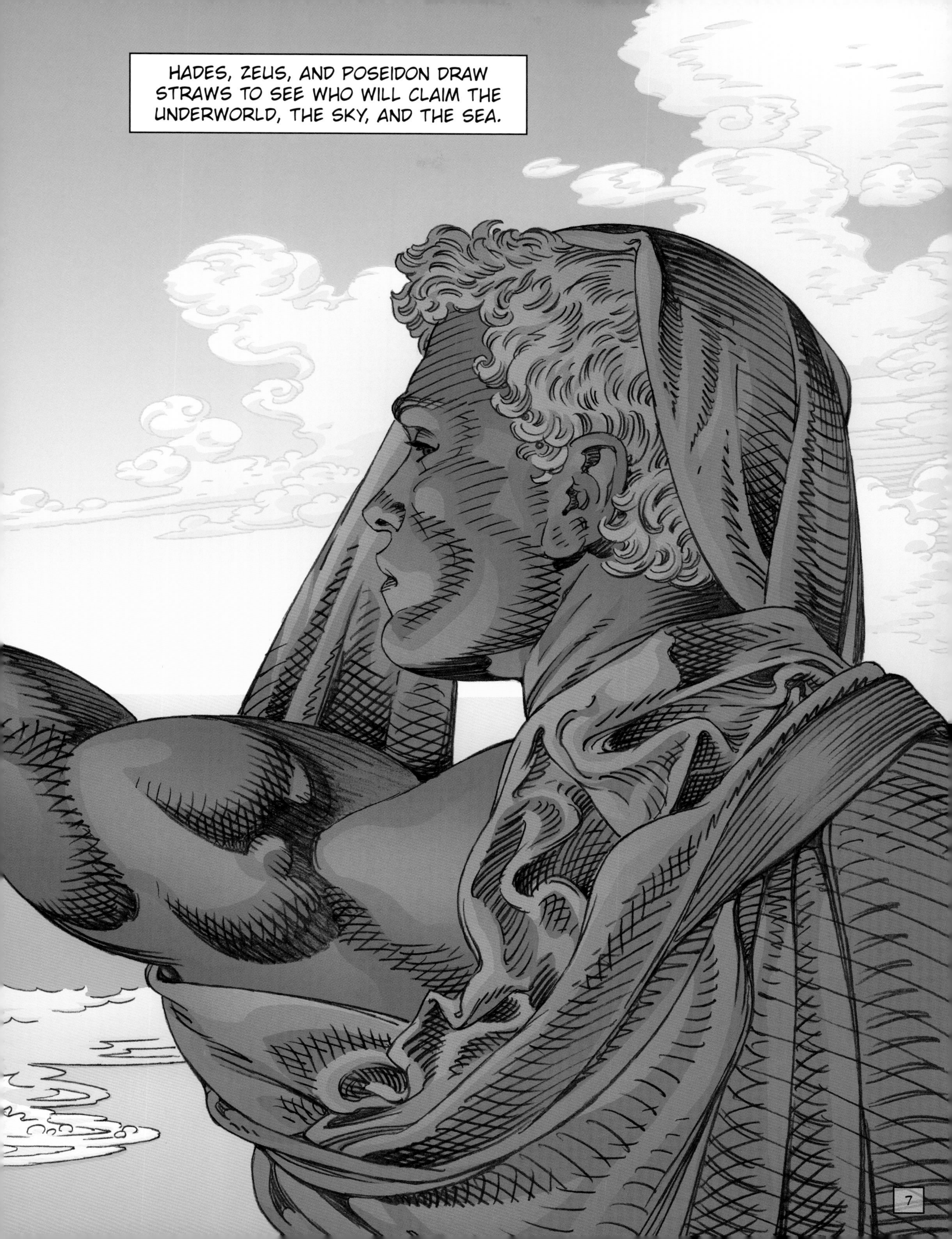
HADES, ZEUS, AND POSEIDON DRAW STRAWS TO SEE WHO WILL CLAIM THE UNDERWORLD, THE SKY, AND THE SEA.

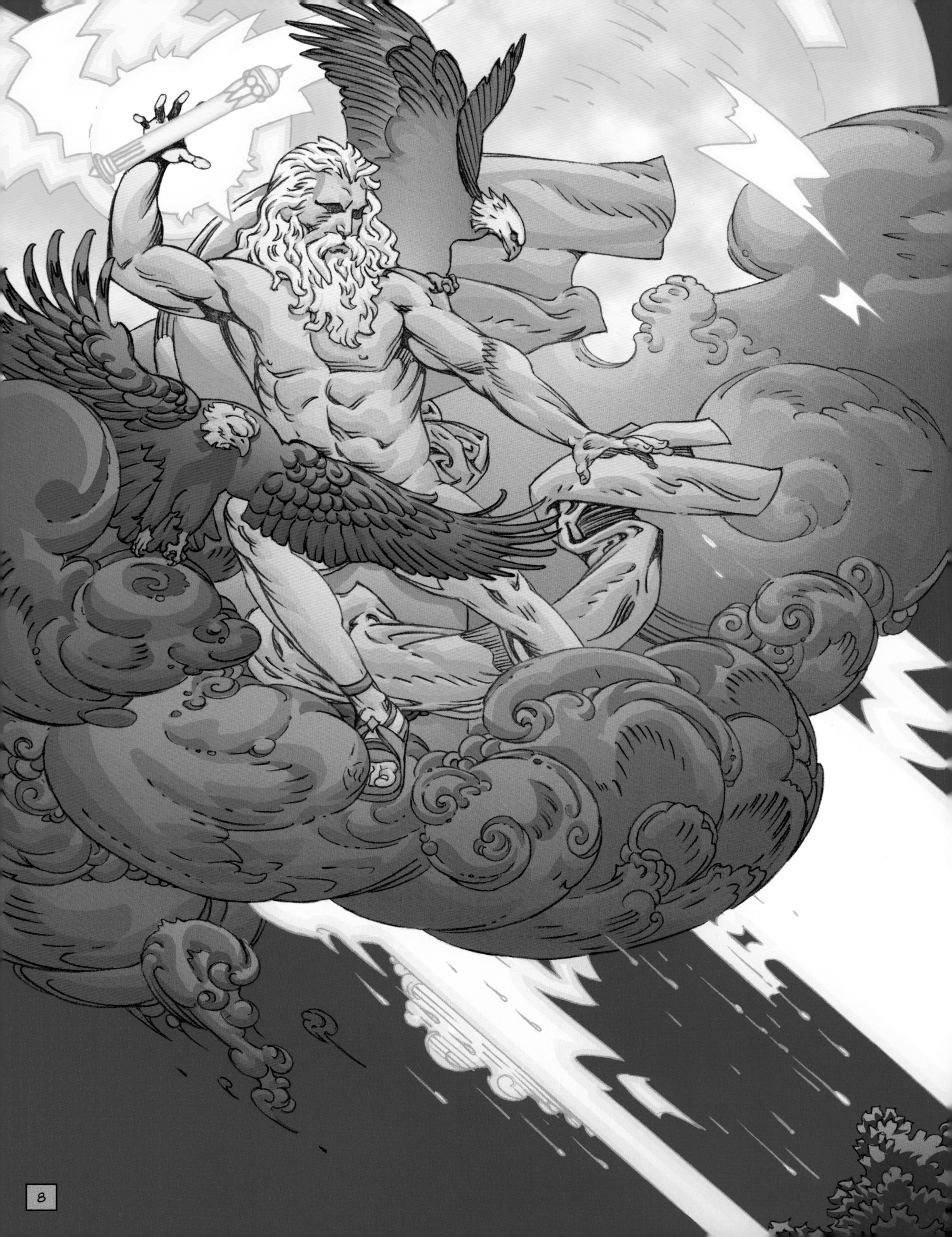

ZEUS
GOD OF ALL GODS

PERCHED ABOVE CLOUDS
MAJESTIC AND HIGH
SITS MIGHTY GOD *ZEUS*,
LORD SUPREME OF THE SKY.
SURVEYING MERE MORTALS
FROM A GOLD MARBLED THRONE,
ABLAZE IN GLORY
ATOP HIS MOUNT OLYMPUS HOME.
CONSPIRING
AND *TESTING*
WITH BALD EAGLES RESTING
ON MOUNTAINOUS SHOULDERS
HE DISHES OUT BLESSINGS
TO THOSE WHO ARE WEAK
TO THOSE WHO ARE MEEK
TO THOSE WHO GIVE THANKS
TO THE GODS WHEN THEY SPEAK.
THE RAIN GOD WHO REIGNS
WITH SCEPTER IN HAND
GATHERS UP CLOUDS
TO BLANKET THE LAND,
PREPARING TO *PUNISH*
THOSE WHO TELL *LIES*
AND THOSE WHO REVEAL
WICKED THOUGHTS IN THEIR EYES.
WITH WHITE WHISKERS CURLED
AND RED LIPS UNFURLED
HE EXHALES A HURRICANE BREEZE,
FILLED WITH ANGER

THAT BURSTS THROUGH THE CLOUDS,
SHAKING AND SWAYING THE TREES,
UNLEASHING HIS *WRATH*
ON THOSE WHO DISPLEASE.
THESE MORTALS THEN PRAY
AND DROP TO THEIR KNEES,
AND PLEAD FOR *MERCY*
FOR THEIR ATTEMPTS TO DECEIVE.
BUT PLEAS
AND PRAYERS
FALL ON DEAF EARS
AS ZEUS DROPS TO THE EARTH
A RIVER OF TEARS;
A RIVER OF TEARS
STIRRED BY THE WIND,
SIGNALING PUNISHMENT
FROM ZEUS WILL BEGIN.
RAISING HIS SCEPTER
HIGH TO THE SKY,
HIS RIGHT HAND RELEASES
A FLASH THAT LETS FLY
AN ELECTRICALLY CHARGED
FLAMING THUNDERBOLT
THAT STAGGERS DISHONEST
MORTALS WITH A JOLT,
A JOLT THAT JUMPS
FROM SKIES HE TEARS OPEN,
SINGEING A MESSAGE
THAT SAYS: *"ZEUS HAS SPOKEN!"*

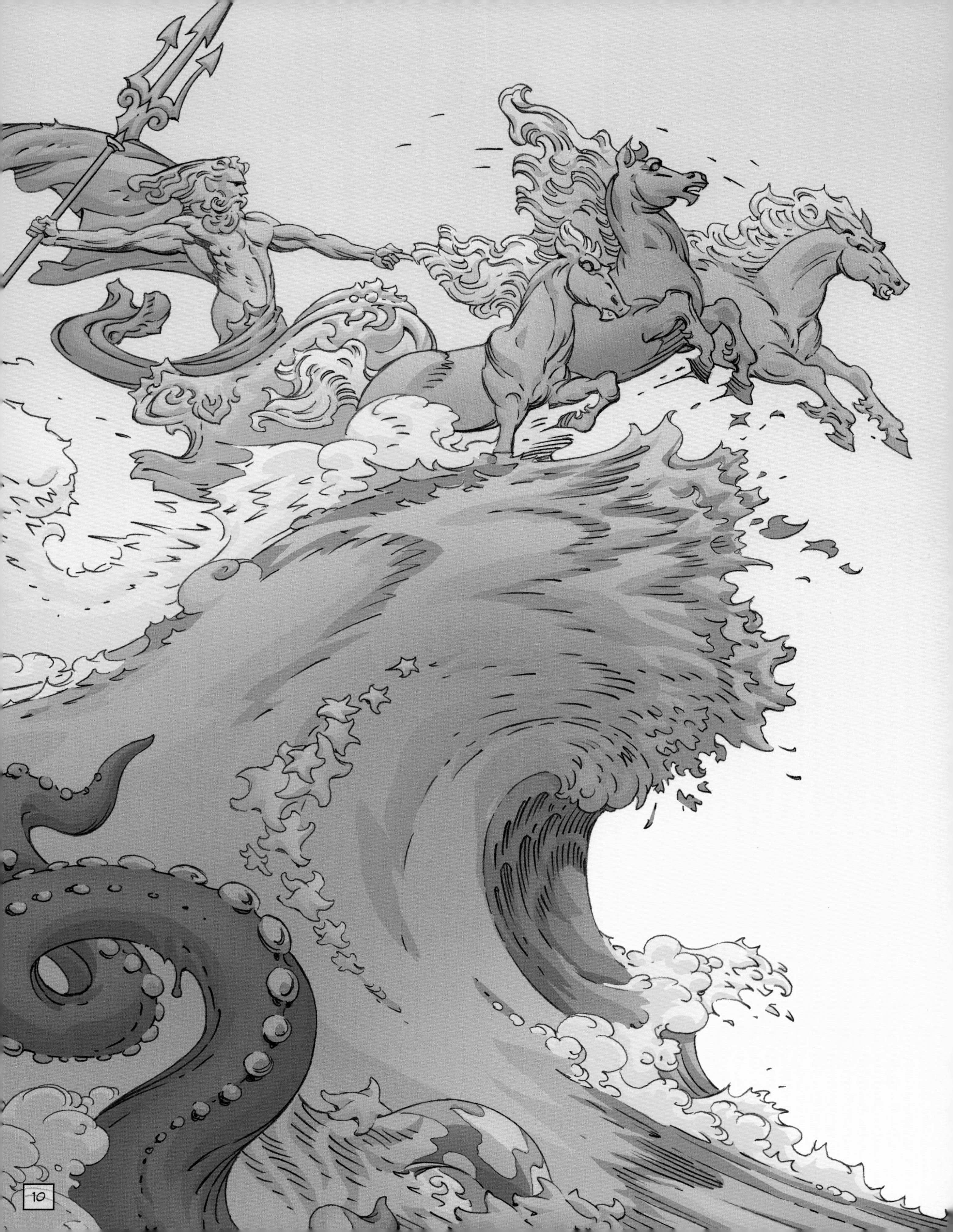

POSEIDON
GOD OF THE SEA

SURFING
AND SKIMMING
AND STRIDING
AND GLIDING
ACROSS OCEAN WAVES
WITH HIS SPEAR, THE TRIDENT,
POSEIDON REIGNS
AS GOD OF THE SEA,
PULLED BY HIS CHARIOT
OF SEA HORSES WITH EASE.
GOLDEN THEY GLOW
AS OCEAN WINDS BLOW,
HIS SEA-BLUE MANE
AND BEARD THAT FLOW
FROM HIS STRONG FACE
FRAMING FIERCE EYES OF BLUE,
SURVEYING THE OCEAN
AND ITS CREATURES, TOO.
BROTHER OF ZEUS,
THE SEA GOD CAN BE
QUICK-TEMPERED
DIFFICULT
JEALOUS
AND ***GREEDY***,
FIGHTING WITH GODS
FOR POSSESSION OF CITIES.
A SORE LOSER IN BATTLE
HE CREATES ENEMIES
AND CONTROLS THE OCEANS
WITH HIS EMOTIONS,
ABLE TO CALM
OR CAUSE GREAT COMMOTION
WITH A GRAND SWEEPING
WAVE OF THE HAND,
STILLING ROUGH WATERS
OR FLOODING DRY LAND.
ANYONE WHO ANGERS
POSEIDON WILL SEE
THE POWER HE HAS
WHEN BROUGHT TO FURY,
WHEN HE RAISES HIGH
TO THE SKY HIS THREE-
PRONGED SPEAR, THE TRIDENT,
AND BRINGS DOWN QUICKLY
HIS SPEAR TO ***SHATTER***
ROCKS AND RUMBLE
THE EARTH AS BUILDINGS
COLLAPSE AND ***CRUMBLE***
FROM WAVE-CRASHING
LAND-SMASHING
TEMPESTUOUS TIDES
MADE BY THE GOD
WHO IN THREE EASY STRIDES
SHAKES UP THE SOIL
AS THE EARTH-QUAKER
THEN DESTROYS IT WITH WATER
AS ***THE STORM-MAKER.***

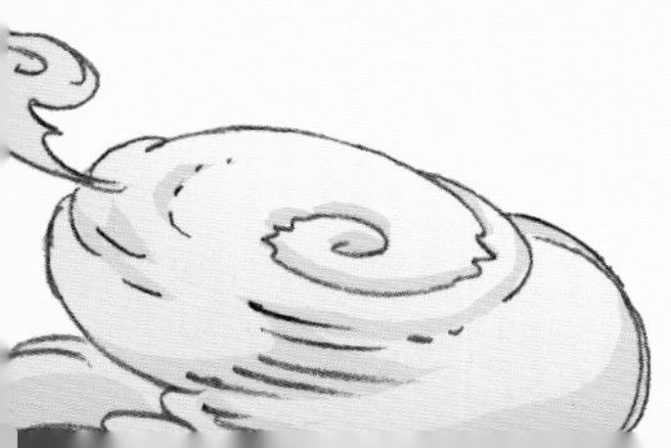

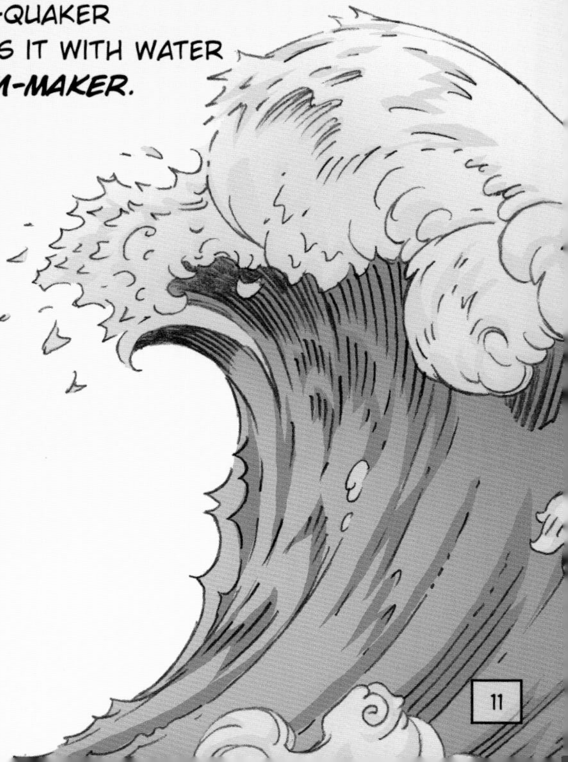

HADES
GOD OF THE UNDERWORLD

IN A LAND MORTALS DREAD
WHERE EVEN GODS FEAR TO TREAD
LIVES *HADES*, THE GOD
OF THE UNDERWORLD AND DEAD,
SURVEYING HIS VAST
SUNLESS DOMAIN,
LORD OF A WORLD
SHARING HIS NAME,
WHERE GHOSTLY FLOWERS
DOT GHOSTLY MEADOWS,
SNIPPED AND SNIFFED
BY SPIRITS AND SHADOWS.
HIDDEN BENEATH EARTH
THE GOD ALSO KNOWN
AS *THE RICH ONE* SITS
ON A BLACK MARBLED THRONE,
SURROUNDED BY JEWELS
AND PRECIOUS STONES,
WITH HIS KIDNAPPED
WIFE, PERSEPHONE,
SNATCHED
FROM THE EARTH
BECAUSE OF HER BEAUTY.

VIEWED BY HIS SIBLINGS
AS FRAIL AND WEAK,
THIS OLYMPIAN'S NAME
MORTALS *DARE NOT SPEAK*
FOR FEAR THAT HIS NAME
WHEN GIVEN SOUND
WILL RAISE HADES UP
TO SUMMON THEM DOWN
TO HIS DEAD PALACE GATES,
WHERE HIS THREE-HEADED GUARD DOG,
CERBERUS, AWAITS.
BROTHER OF ZEUS
AND THE SEA GOD POSEIDON,
GRAY-SKINNED HADES
PHYSICALLY *FRIGHTENS*
MORTALS SO HE
HIDES HIS IDENTITY
WITH A HELMET THAT CREATES
INVISIBILITY
TO WALK AMONG THE LIVING
WITH ANTICIPATION
BLESSING WARRIORS WHO MIGHT
INCREASE HIS POPULATION.

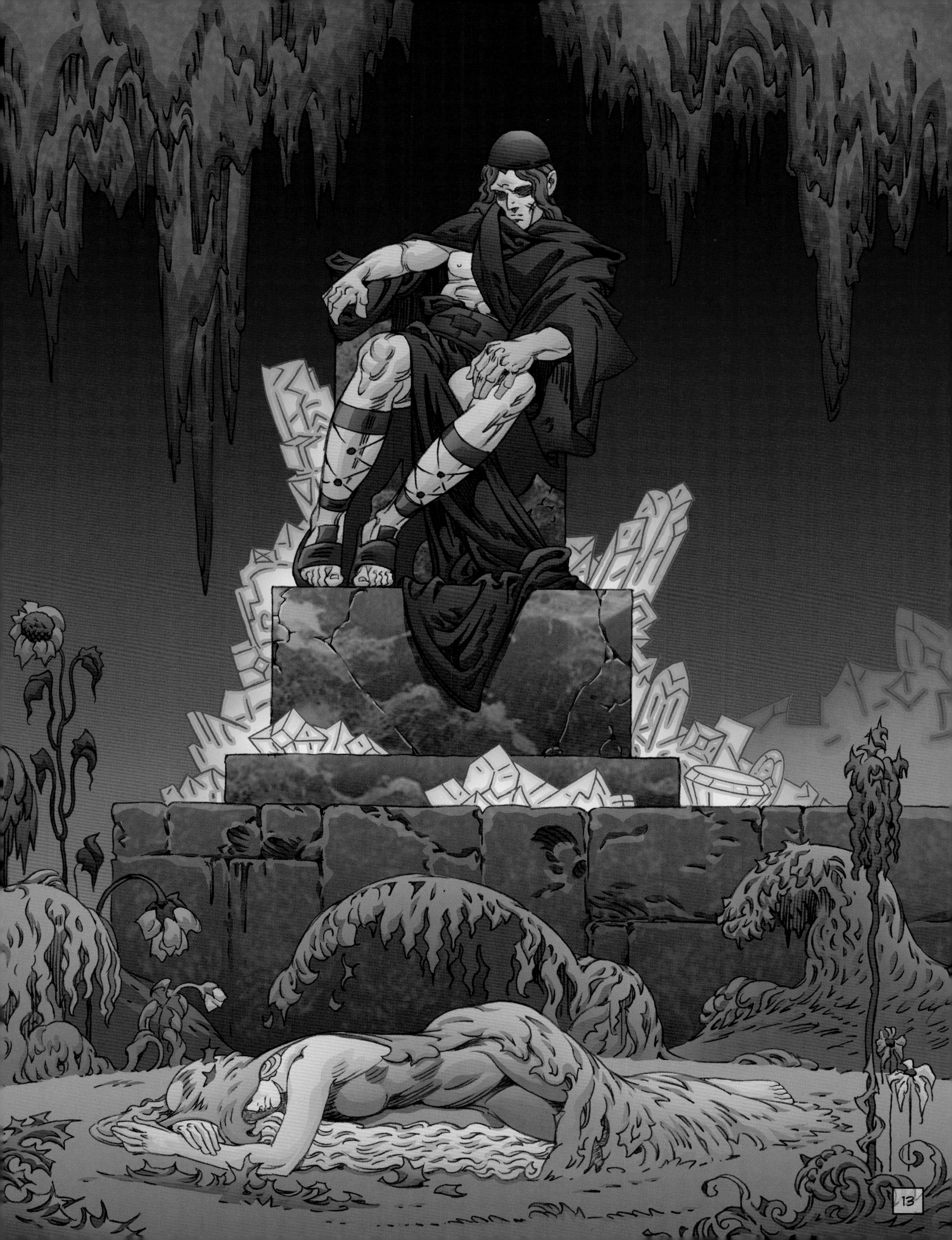

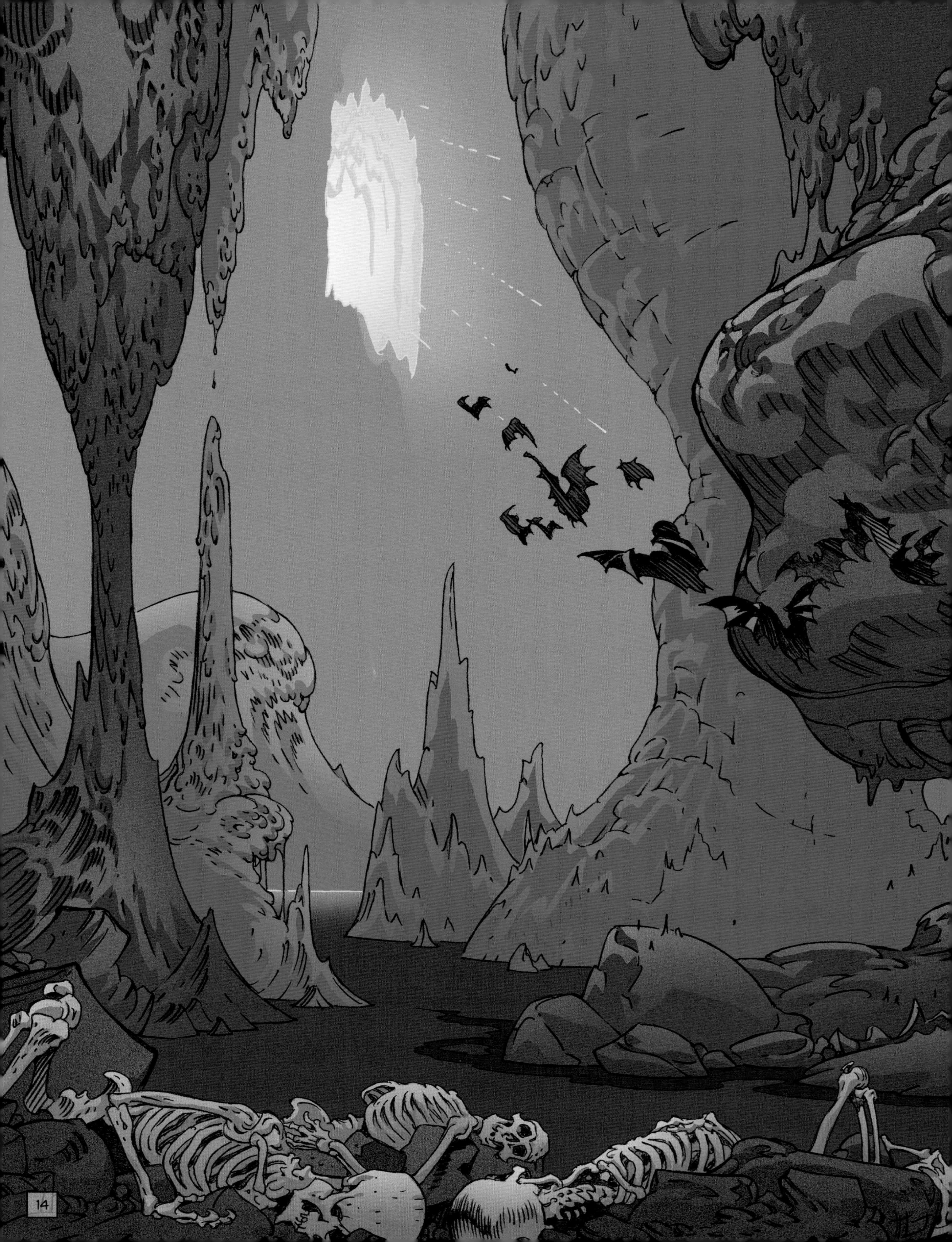

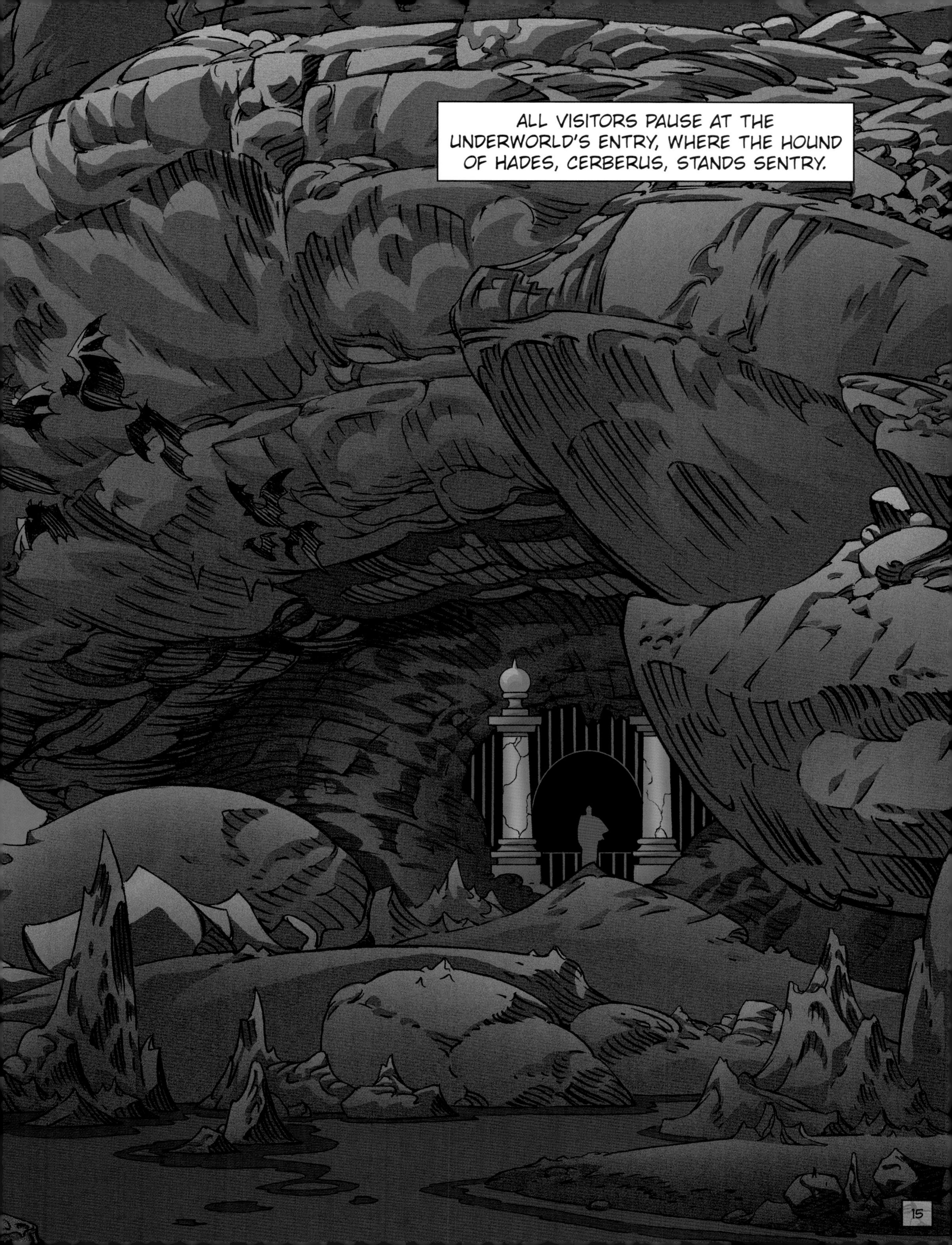
ALL VISITORS PAUSE AT THE UNDERWORLD'S ENTRY, WHERE THE HOUND OF HADES, CERBERUS, STANDS SENTRY.

CERBERUS
GUARD DOG TO THE UNDERWORLD

SNAPPING
SNAPPING
SNAPPING
JAWS
JAWS
JAWS
WITH TEETH LIKE *DAGGERS*
WHILE CLAWS
CLAWS
CLAWS
MAKE ALL VISITORS PAUSE
AT THE UNDERWORLD'S ENTRY,
WHERE THE HOUND OF HADES,
CERBERUS, STANDS SENTRY
GUARDING THE LAND
OF THE DEAD WITH THREE
HEADS
SIX EYES
AND ONE FEROCIOUS BODY.
DOGGEDLY FOCUSED
ON NEW SOULS WHO PASS,
EACH HEAD HAS
ITS OWN SPECIFIC TASK.
WITH FLOP EARS, SAD EYES,
AND A QUIVERING NOSE,
THE HOUND HEAD ON THE LEFT
KEEPS AWAY THOSE
LIVING WHO WANT

ACCESS AND ENTRY
BUT *BLOOD-STAINED* FANGS
FORCE THEM TO FLEE.
WOLFLIKE EARS
AND DARK, GLOWING EYES
ON THE MIDDLE HEAD FOCUS,
UNBLINKING, TO SPY
ON ANYONE WHO
CONTINUES TO TRY
TO ESCAPE THE UNDERWORLD
WHILE THE HEAD ON THE RIGHT,
A *SNARLING* BULL TERRIER
POP-EYED AND SKULL-LIKE,
SNAPS HIS JAWS
AND EXPOSES HIS TEETH
WITH *BLACK POISON* FOAMING,
ANXIOUS TO *EAT*
THOSE WHO ATTEMPT
AN UNDERWORLD EXIT,
DEVOURING ALL
WHO FAIL IN THEIR QUEST,
PROVING
THE HOUND
WITH EYES
FLASH-FLASH-FLASHING RED
TAKES ADVANTAGE OF EACH
SNARL-SNARL-SNARLING HEAD.

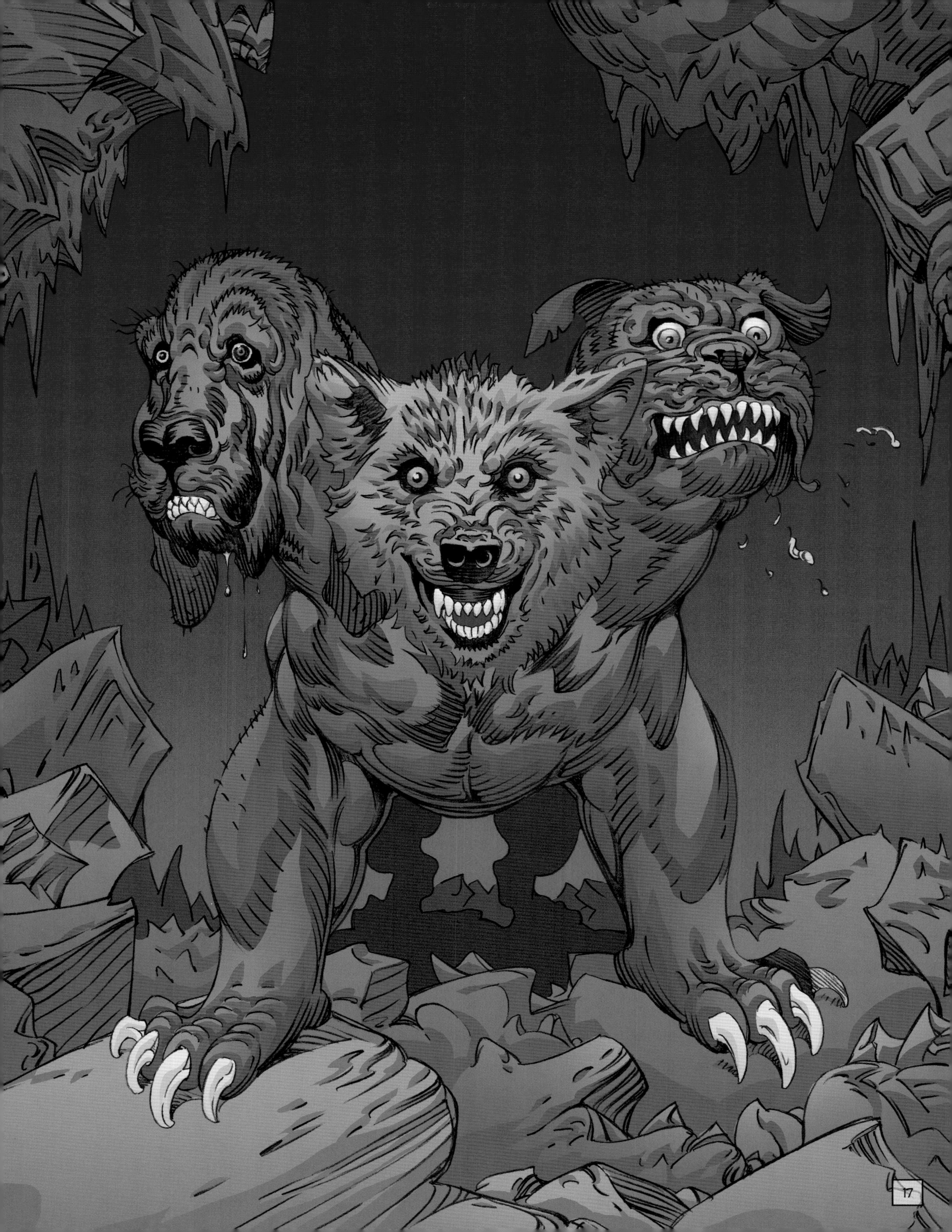

HERMES
MESSENGER OF THE GODS

RACING THE WIND
IN GOLD-WINGED SANDALS
MOVES HARE-FOOTED *HERMES*,
THE GOD WHO HANDLES
ALL COMMANDS GIVEN
FROM THE MOUTH OF ZEUS,
WHO SETS IN MOTION
THE MESSENGER'S SHOES
AS HE CARRIES HIS STAFF,
ENCIRCLED WITH TWO
SLITHERING SNAKES,
WHEREVER HE FLEW.
QUICK-WITTED, CUNNING,
WITH A MOUTH PRONE TO LIES,
HIS DELIVERY DUTIES
KEEP HIM OCCUPIED.
A *TRICKSTER* WHOSE CLEVER
MIND FROM DAY ONE
WAS PUT ON DISPLAY
WHEN BORN ZEUS'S SON:
INVENTING THE LYRE,

AN INSTRUMENT WITH STRINGS
STRUNG TO A TORTOISE SHELL
THAT, WHEN PLUCKED, SINGS
AND SOOTHES
AND RELAXES
AND CALMS
THE SOUL,
AND HIS INVENTION
SAVED HIM WHEN HE STOLE
APOLLO'S CATTLE
AT JUST THREE HOURS YOUNG;
A *PRECOCIOUS* INFANT
JUST LOOKING FOR FUN.
THE QUICK-THINKING TOT
AND FUTURE GOD OF THIEVES
ERASED HIS FOOTPRINTS
WITH BRANCHES AND LEAVES
AND HID THE HERD,
BUT APOLLO KNEW
HIS PRIZED BOVINES WERE WITH
THE *YOUNG BANDIT* WHO

PRETENDED TO BE
AN INNOCENT BABY
ROUSING THE GOD
OF MUSIC'S FURY.
PLUCKING THE STRINGS
OF HIS SWEET-SINGING LYRE,
HERMES COOLED
APOLLO'S FIRE
AND OFFERED THE INSTRUMENT
TO HIM AS A GIFT
IN EXCHANGE FOR THE COWS
AND ENDED THEIR RIFT.
THIEVES, GAMBLERS,
TRADERS, AND TRAVELERS
ALL HONOR HERMES
THE ***MISCHIEVOUS*** MESSENGER
WHOSE WELL-TRAVELED SOLES
SERVE ANOTHER ROLE,
FOR HADES AS
THE CONDUCTOR OF SOULS,
ESCORTING THE ***DEAD***
TO THE UNDERWORLD GATES,
WHERE HADES LORDS OVER
THEIR LAST RESTING PLACE.
MUSIC AND MISCHIEF
OCCUPY HIS TIME,
BUT STREAKING THE SKY
IS WHERE YOU MIGHT FIND
THE FLEET FEET OF HERMES
RIDING THE BREEZE,
DARTING THROUGH CLOUDS
LIKE AN ARROW THROUGH LEAVES.

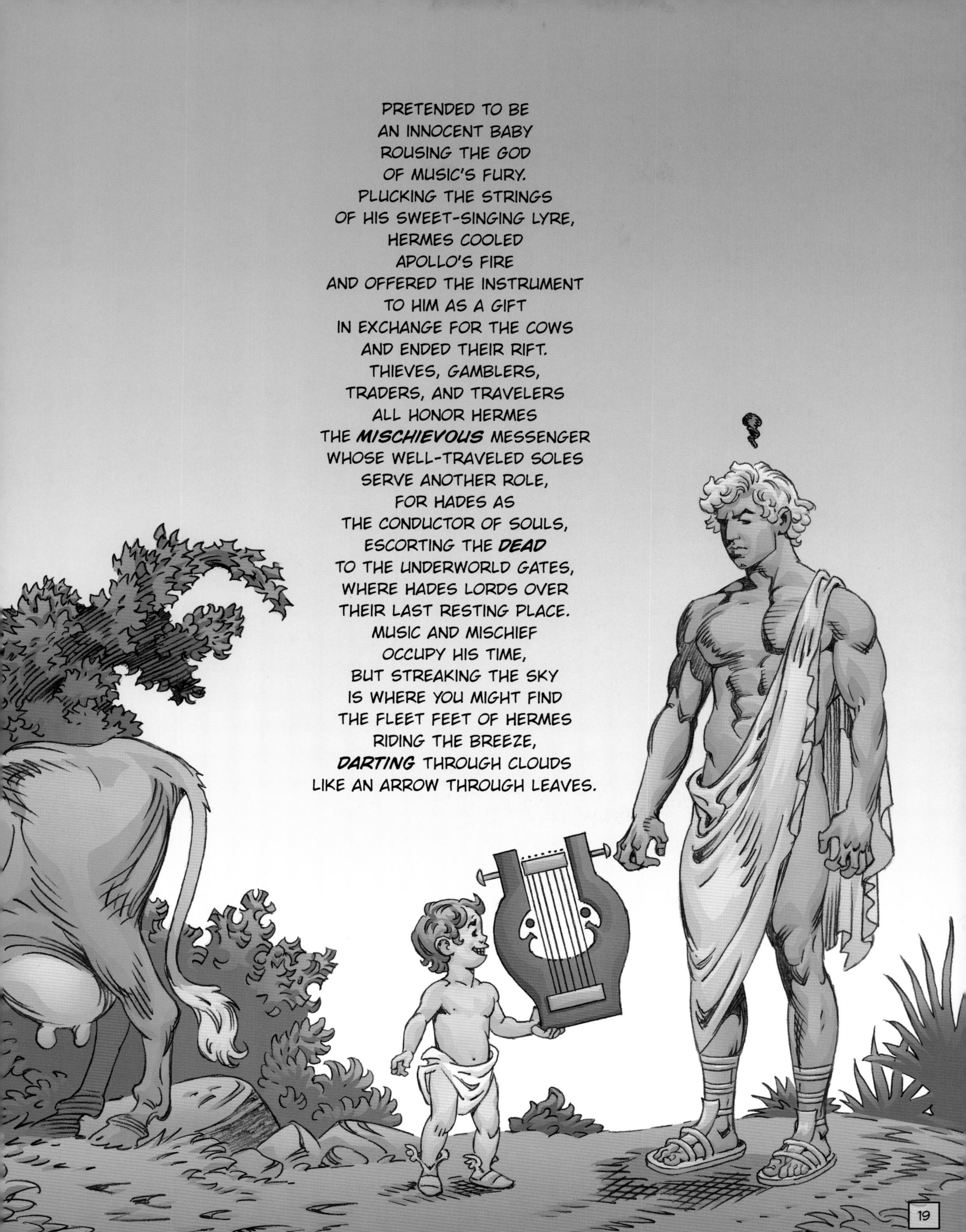

ARTEMIS AND APOLLO, THE TWINS, CAN BE FOUND ON EARTH SLINGING ARROWS WITHOUT BEING HEARD AND WITHOUT BEING SEEN.

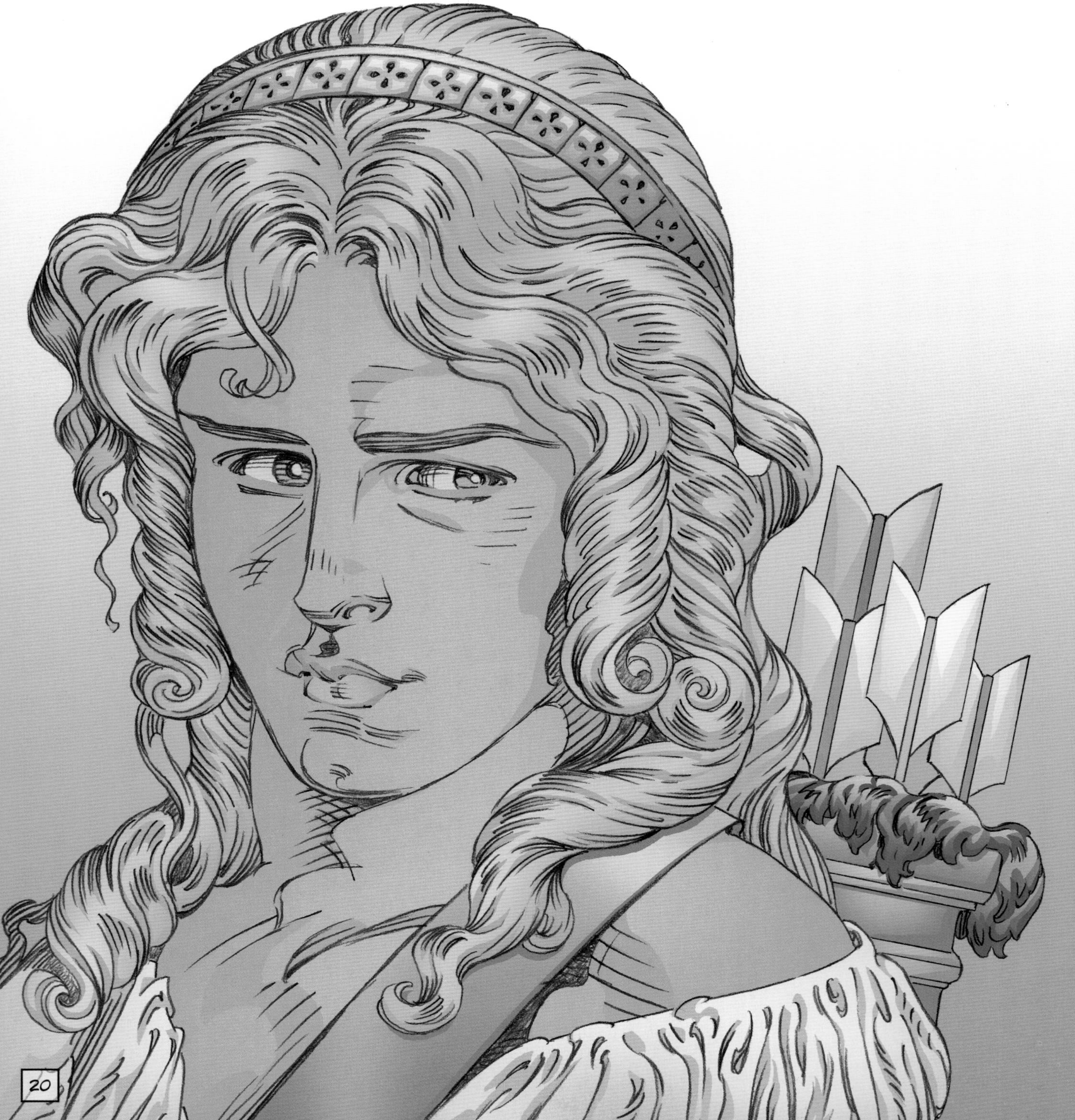

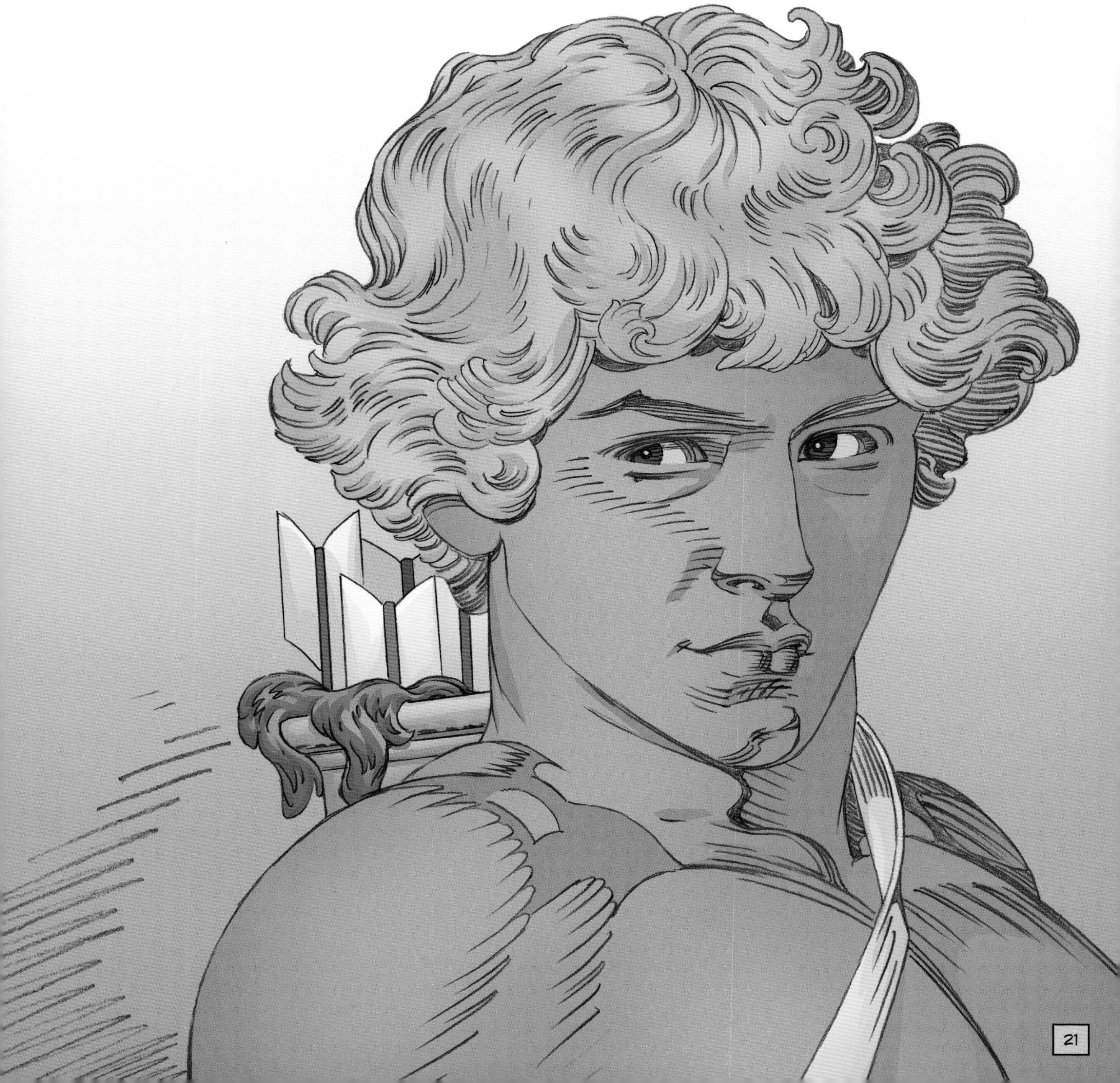

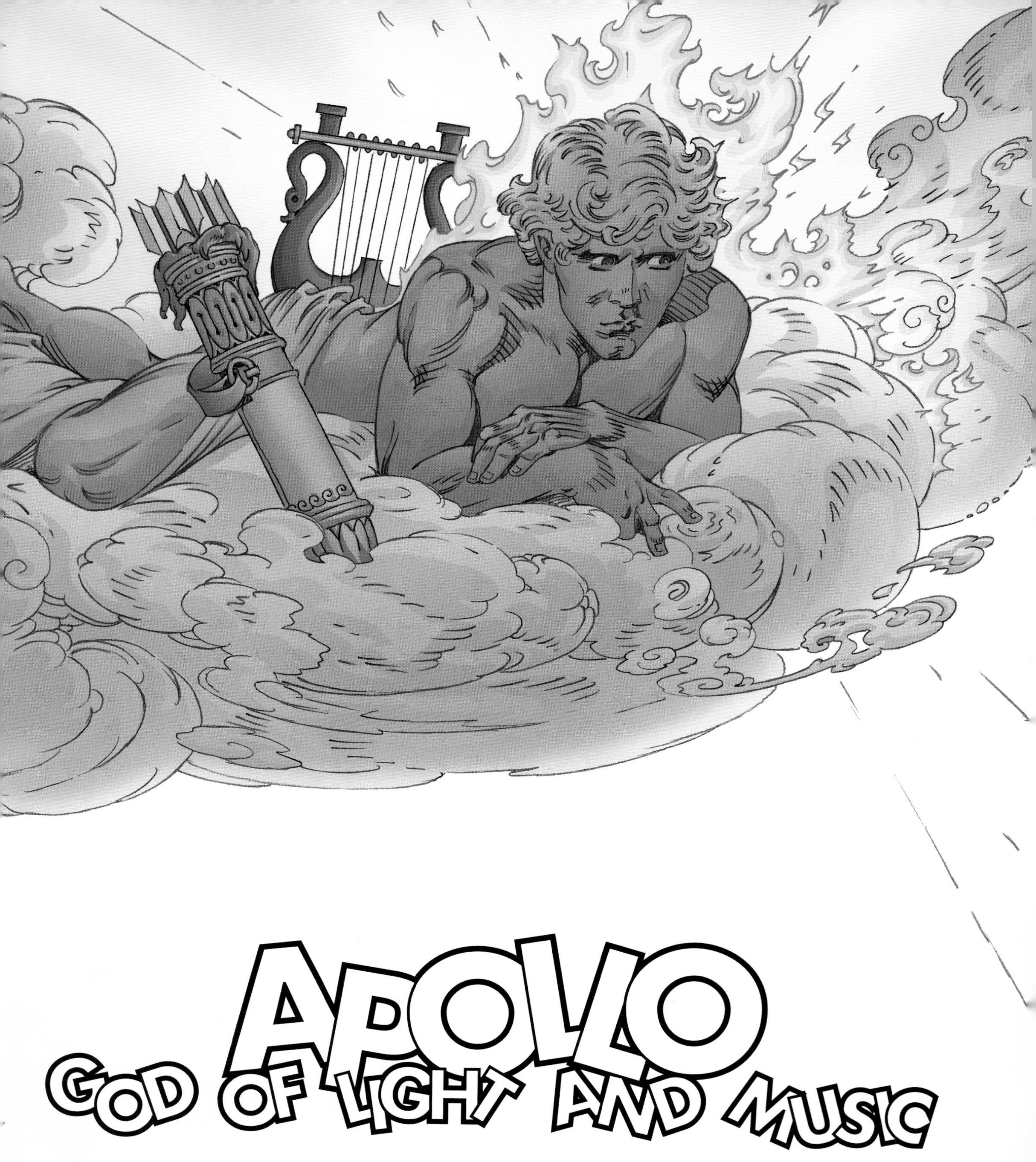

APOLLO
GOD OF LIGHT AND MUSIC

BRIGHT AS THE SUN
GLOWING GOLD, SCORCHING SIGHT,
STANDS ***APOLLO***, THE GOD OF
ART, MUSIC, AND LIGHT,
WITH ***BRILLIANT*** BLOND CURLS
AND ***RADIANT*** EYES,
THE GOD OF TRUTH
WHO CANNOT TELL LIES
BUT CAN ENCHANT EARS
WITH HIS LYRE THAT SINGS
SWEET MUSIC FROM SOFT
FINGERTIPS PLUCKING STRINGS.
TWIN BROTHER OF ARTEMIS,
SON OF ZEUS AND LETO,
APOLLO SHOOTS ARROWS
AS LORD OF THE SILVER BOW,
USING FEATHERY FINGERS
TO PRECISELY GUIDE
FAR-REACHING ARROWS
THAT GLIDE AND RIDE
THE WIND AND PIERCE
LIKE RAYS OF THE SUN
THOSE WHO INSULT
OR OPPOSE THE BRIGHT ONE,
MASTER OF MUSIC,
ARCHERY, AND POETRY,
THE ONLY GOD GIVEN
THE GIFT OF ***PROPHECY***.
DRAWING MORTALS AND MONARCHS
FROM COUNTRIES WORLDWIDE,
HE FORETELLS THE FUTURE
NEAR HIS HOME OF DELPHI.
THOUGHTFUL AND POETIC
APOLLO CAN BE,
OR VENGEFUL AND CRUEL
WHEN FILLED WITH ***FURY***.
KNOWN TO UNLEASH
FROM HIS ***MERCILESS*** HAND
A PLAGUE OF MICE
ON ANIMALS AND MAN,
HE DECIMATES CITIES
OF RULERS WHO LIE,
CHEAT,
STEAL,
AND SCHEME TO DEFY
APOLLO,
THE ARCHER,
GOD OF LIGHT, MUSIC, AND ART,
WHO REVEALS
WHEN ANGERED
THE DARK SIDE OF HIS HEART.

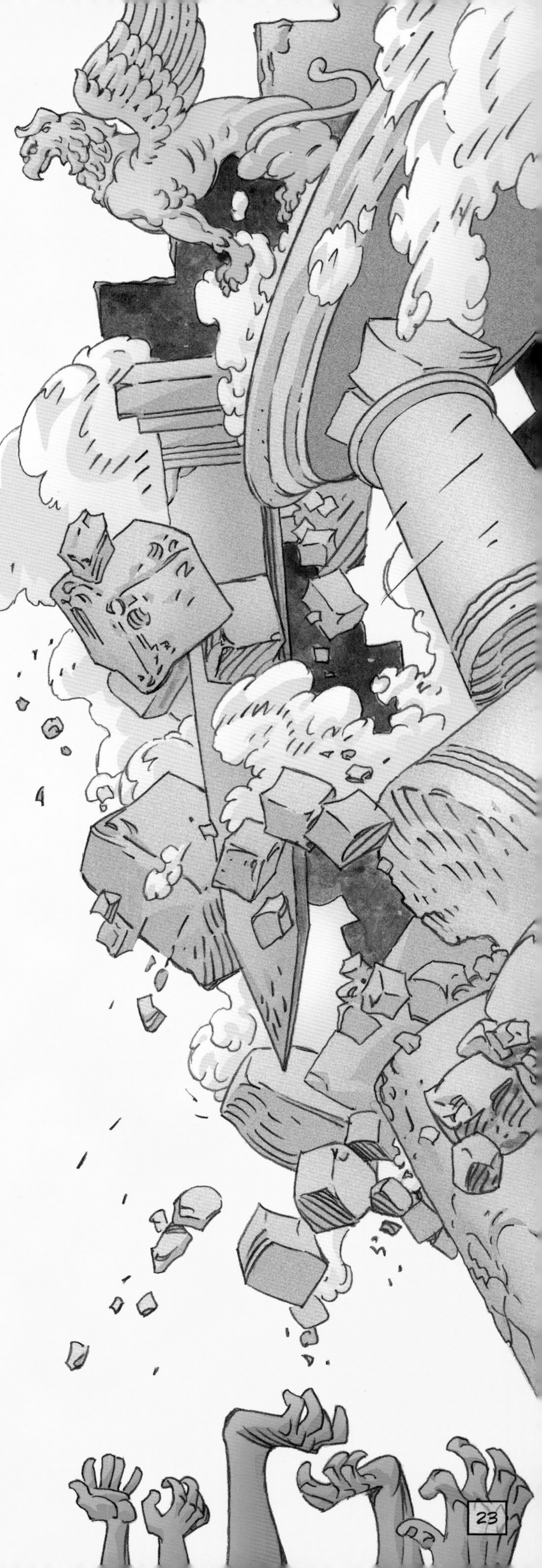

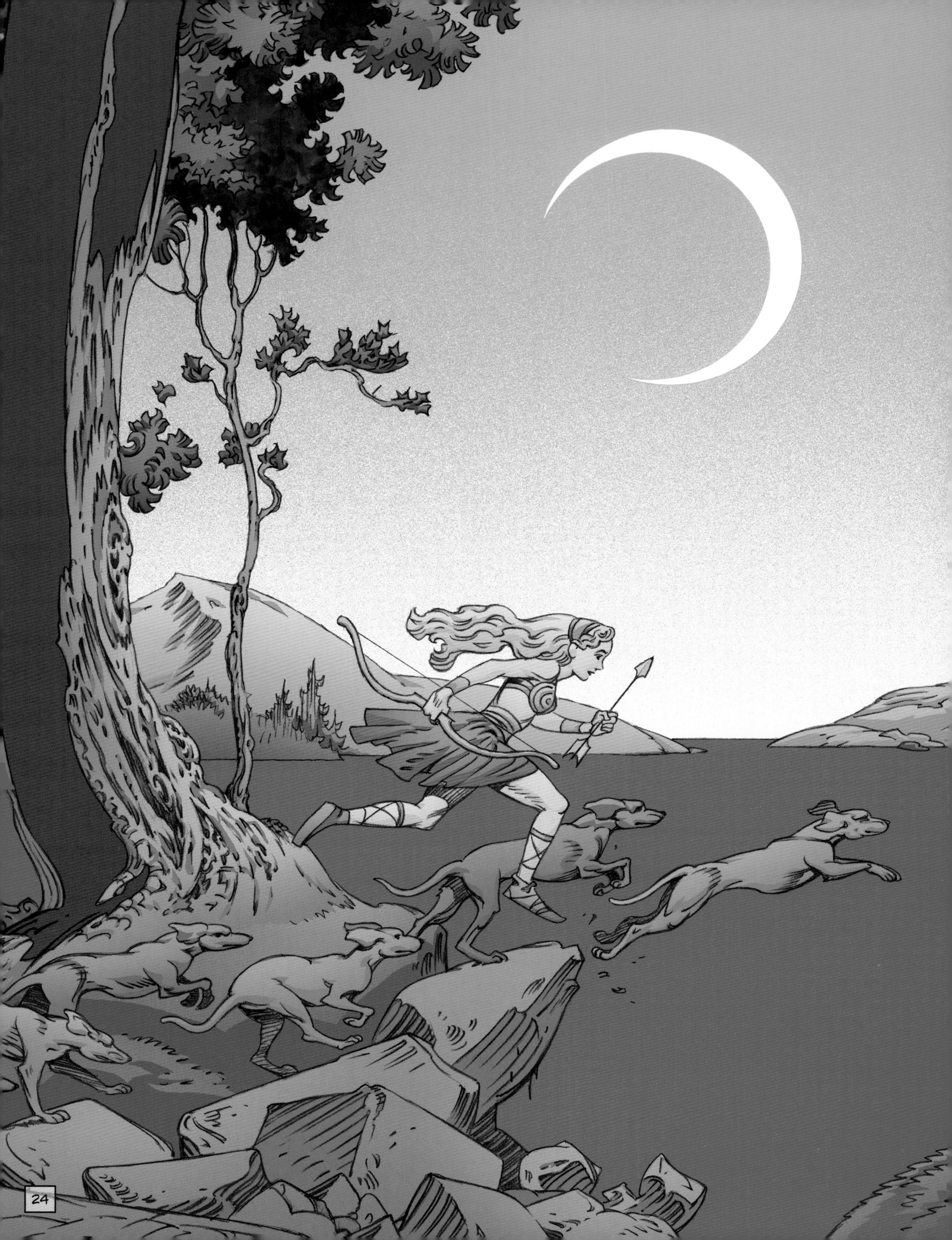

ARTEMIS
GODDESS OF THE HUNT AND MOON

UNDER A SICKLE MOON
STANDS THE GODDESS WHO GLOWS,
ARTEMIS THE HUNTRESS
SLINGING SILVER ARROWS
STRAPPED IN A QUIVER
SLUNG OVER HER BACK,
STEPPING OVER MOUNTAIN
CREVICES AND CRACKS.
HUNTER OF THE GODS
AND GODDESS OF THE MOON,
THE LADY OF WILD THINGS
MOVES IN MAROON.
HER RED TUNIC REACHES
JUST ABOVE HER KNEES
AND EACH ARROW SHOT
SENDS A WHISPER OF BREEZE
THROUGH FORESTS AND TREES
IN THE GREEK COUNTRYSIDE,
WHERE THE SILVER-HAIRED GODDESS
IS KNOWN TO RESIDE.
DAUGHTER OF ZEUS
AND THE TITANESS LETO,
TWIN SISTER OF THE GOD
OF LIGHT, APOLLO,
SHE TRAVELS THROUGH VALLEYS
AND HILLS THAT ECHO,
CLUTCHING HER BOW,
STALKING WITHOUT FEAR,

PURSUING HER PREY
WITH LEGS LIKE A DEER.
SILENT AND *SWIFT*
IN SANDALS SHE STRIDES,
WITH LOP-EARED HOUNDS
ALWAYS AT HER SIDE
TRACKING ANIMALS AND
THOSE MORTALS WHO
ANGER ARTEMIS
AND THE OTHER GODS, TOO.
PRIDEFUL KINGS,
BOASTFUL QUEENS,
AND MEN WHO SPY,
TRYING NOT TO BE SEEN,
WILL FEEL THE PAIN
HER COLD HEART CAN BRING
WHEN SHE PULLS AN ARROW
ACROSS HER BOW
AND ALLOWS *NO PITY*
OR *MERCY* TO SHOW.
AS SHE UNLEASHES
HER FURY IN FLIGHT,
SHE *PIERCES* HER TARGET
WITH EAGLE-EYED SIGHT,
THEN MOUNTING HER CHARIOT
BENEATH A SICKLE MOON'S LIGHT,
HER SILVER STAGS SHOOT
OFF INTO THE NIGHT.

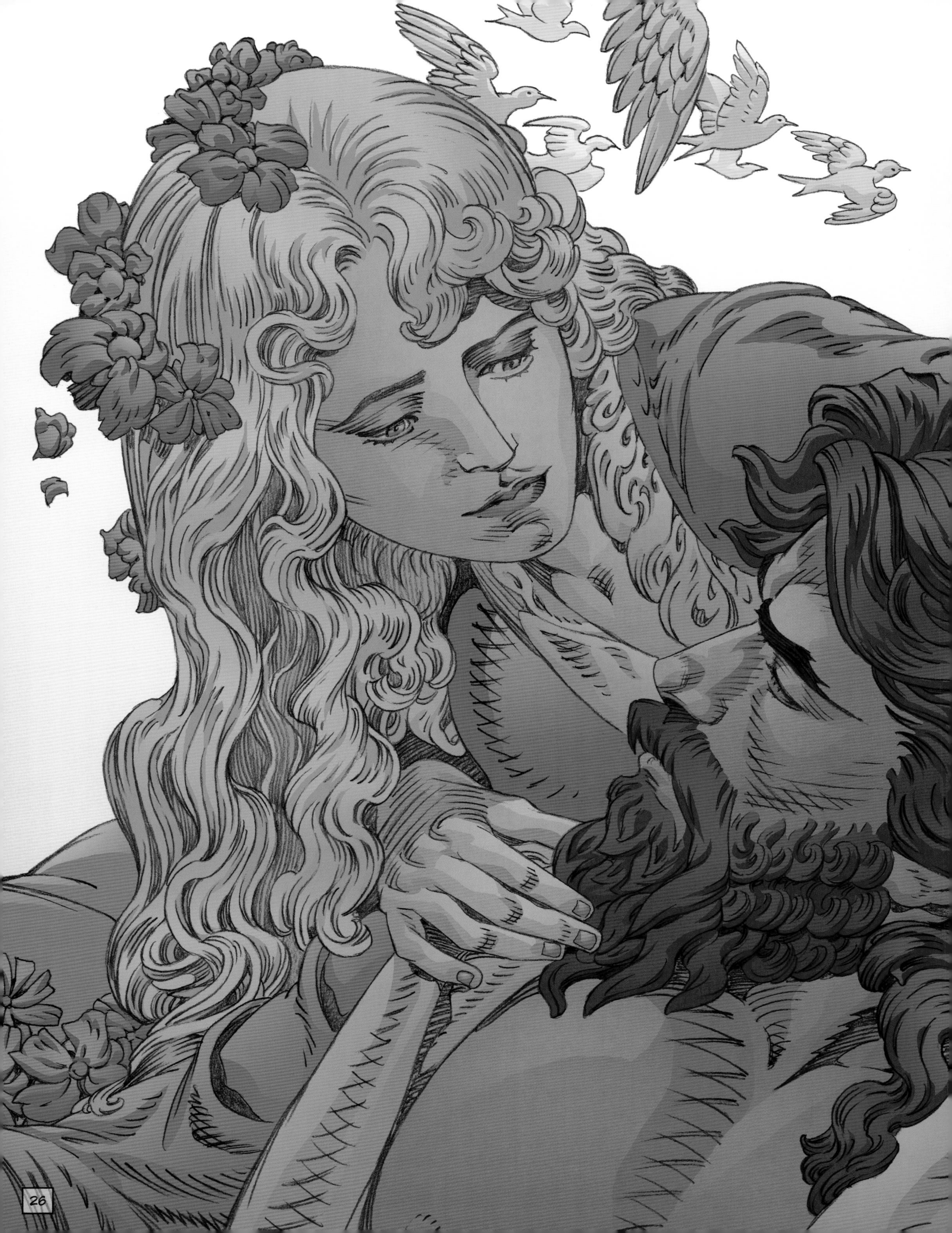

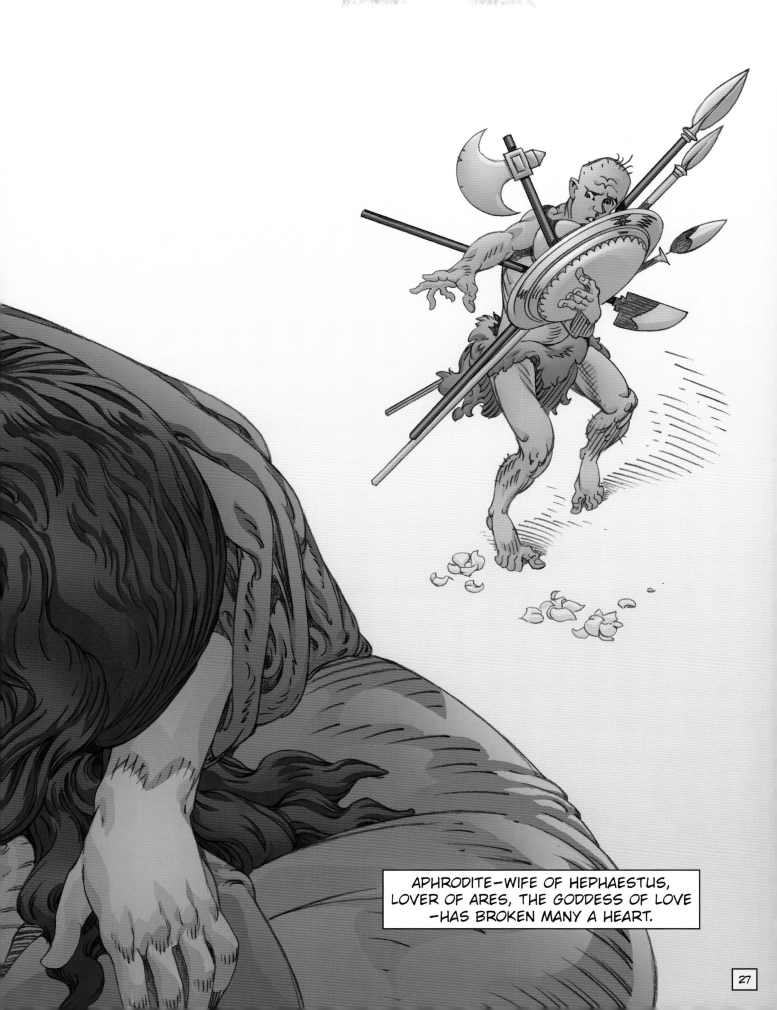

APHRODITE—WIFE OF HEPHAESTUS,
LOVER OF ARES, THE GODDESS OF LOVE
—HAS BROKEN MANY A HEART.

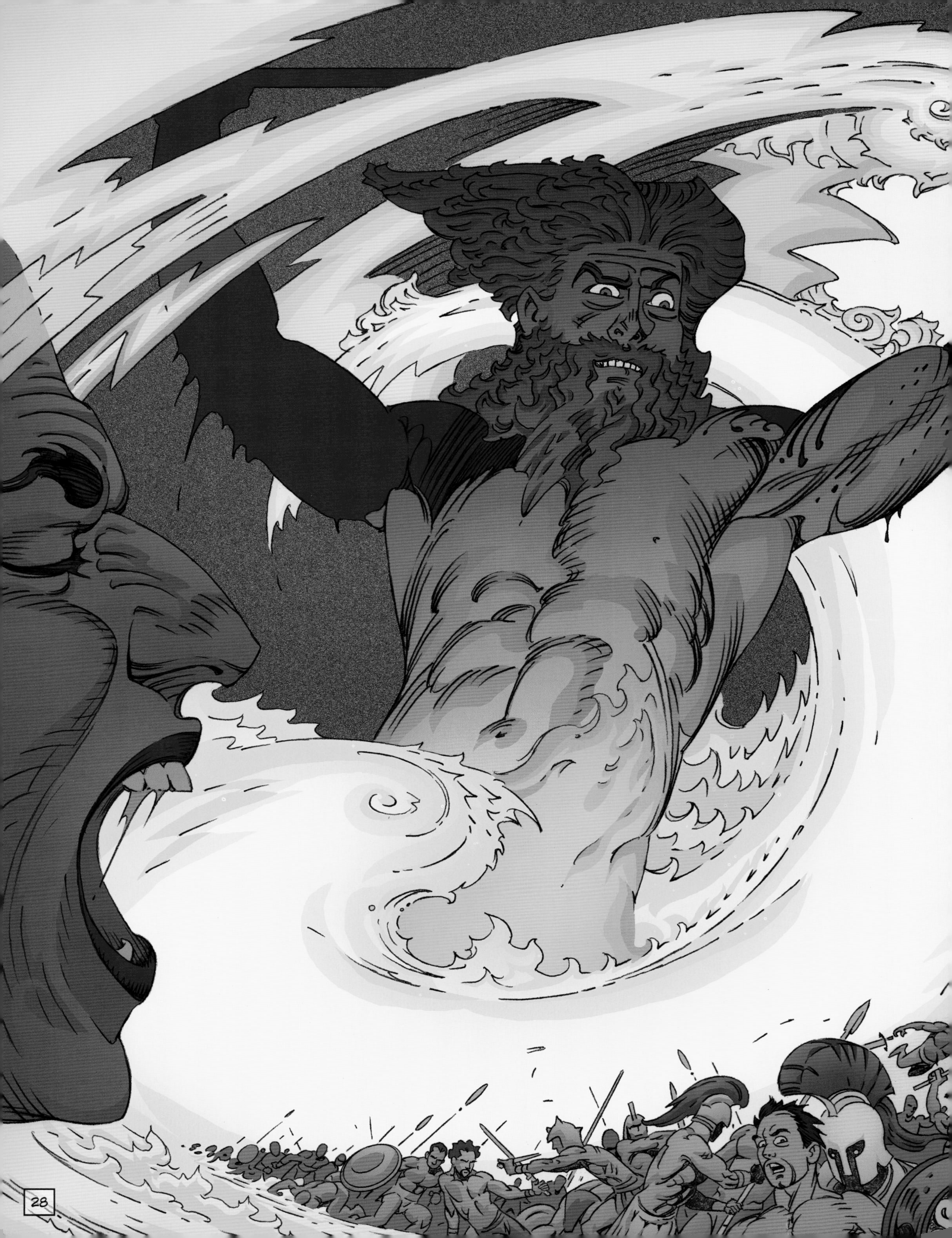

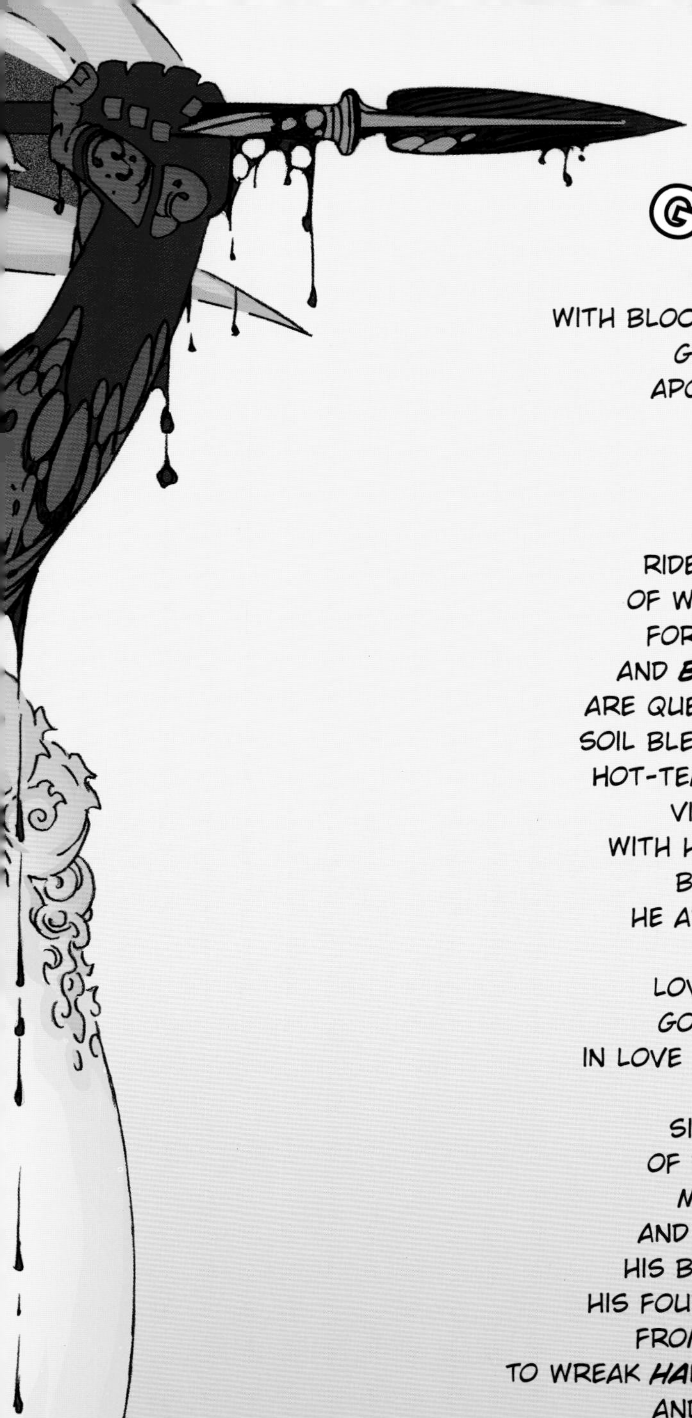

ARES
GOD OF WAR AND STRIFE

SWOOPING DOWN
WITH BLOODTHIRSTY FORCES,
GALLOPING ON FOUR
APOCALYPTIC HORSES,
TERROR
TROUBLE
FLAME
AND FIRE,
RIDES ***ARES***, THE GOD
OF WAR, WHOSE DESIRE
FOR BODIES IN BATTLE
AND ***BLOOD*** TO BE SHED
ARE QUENCHED ONLY WHEN
SOIL BLEEDS CRIMSON RED.
HOT-TEMPERED AND RUDE,
VIOLENT AND VIEWED
WITH HATRED AND SCORN
BY HIS OWN BROOD,
HE ATTRACTED THE EYE
OF AN UNLIKELY
LOVER, THE ALLURING
GODDESS APHRODITE,
IN LOVE WITH THE BRUTISH
GOD OF WAR, WHO
SITS ON HIS THRONE
OF BRASS WAITING TO
MOUNT HIS CHARIOT
AND RAISE TO THE SKY
HIS BURNING TORCH, SO
HIS FOUR HORSES CAN FLY
FROM MOUNT OLYMPUS
TO WREAK ***HAVOC*** AND ***MAYHEM***
AND TO SPREAD PANIC
THROUGHOUT PEACEFUL NATIONS.
HIS TWIN SISTER, DISCORD,
STANDS AT HIS SIDE
SCREECHING SHRILL SCREAMS
AS HIS CHARIOT RIDES
THE WIND AND LANDS
AS HE STEPS OUT TO TREAD
HIS SOLES ON SOIL,
LEAVING A TRAIL OF ***DEAD***,
MERCILESS VOICES
GROANING FOR
BLOOD TO BE SPILLED
AS ARES SHRIEKS:
WARRRR!!!
JOINED BY HIS SONS
TERROR AND FEAR
THE BARBARIC GOD
ENCOURAGES SPEARS
AND BATTLEAXES
TO RAISE HIGH AND CLASH
IN COMBAT TO BRING
JOY TO THE BRASH
WARMONGER WHO REVELS
IN ***CARNAGE*** AND ***CONFLICT***
BUT WAILS LIKE A BABY
WHEN WOUNDED OR HIT
BECAUSE ARES IS SIMPLY
A COWARDLY BULLY,
NEITHER FEARSOME
NOR FEARLESS
NOR STRONG
NOR SAVVY.
AND YOU CAN FIND
HIS SHAMED AND BLOODSTAINED
BODY CRAWLING BACK
TO OLYMPUS IN PAIN.

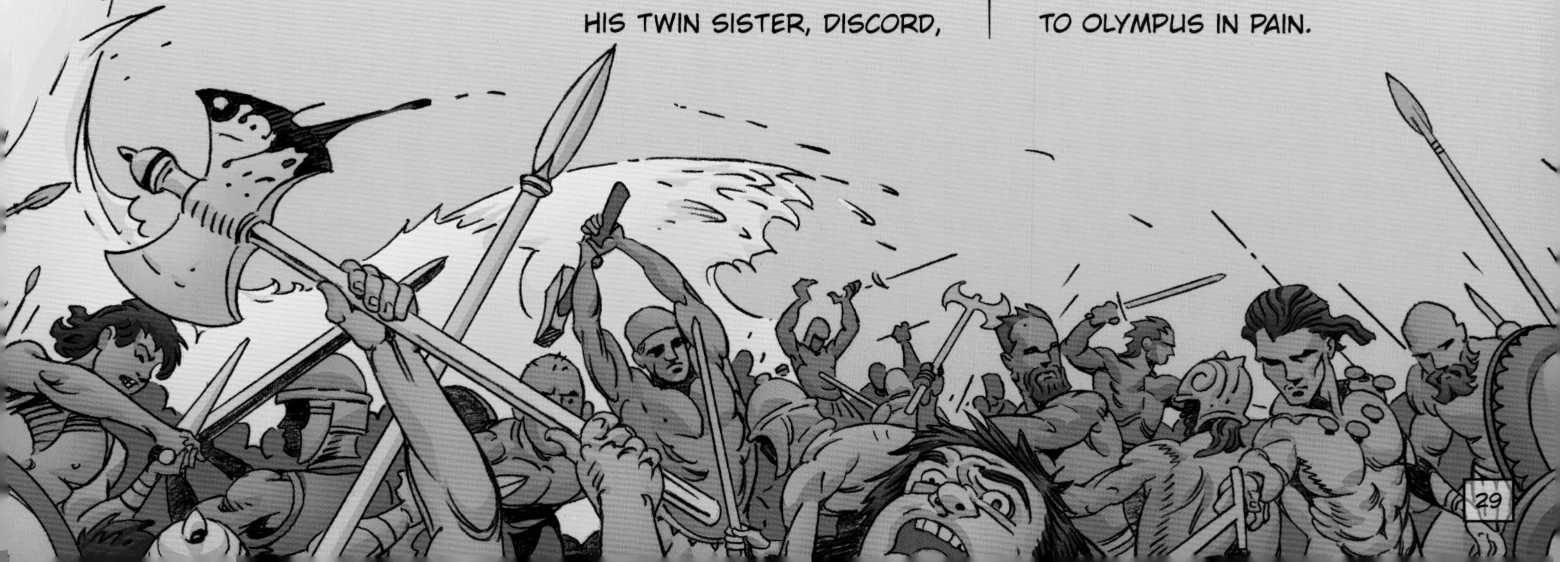

APHRODITE
GODDESS OF LOVE AND BEAUTY

BUBBLING WITH LAUGHTER
FROM THE FOAM OF THE SEA
RISES THE GODDESS OF LOVE
AND BEAUTY, *APHRODITE.*
IMMENSELY IRRESISTIBLE
BEWITCHINGLY BEAUTIFUL
PASSIONATELY PEERLESS
IN A MAGICAL GIRDLE
GRACING HER FORM
ADORNING HER WAIST
FORCING ALL EYES
TO FOCUS ON HER FACE;
SHE HARNESSES HEARTS
TO FILL THEM WITH FIRE
AND COMPELS ANYONE
SHE WISHES TO DESIRE HER.
DAUGHTER OF THE SEA,
WAVES LAUGH,
SMILE,
AND CRASH
WHEN CREATURES OF THE SEA
WITNESS APHRODITE PASS.
SONGBIRDS SING SWEETLY
AND ENCIRCLE HER HAIR
AS SALT WATER AND SAND
TURN CHIVALROUS IN THEIR
TEMPESTUOUS TIDE,
ALLOWING HER TO TAKE
SOFT STEPS AS SHE LEAVES
FRESH FLOWERS IN HER WAKE
IN A PARADE OF COLORS
FOLLOWING HER FEET,
STITCHING THE SOIL

WHERE IMMORTAL TOES MEET.
MOTHER OF EROS
WIFE OF HEPHAESTUS
LOVER OF ARES
AND SOMETIMES TREACHEROUS,
THE GODDESS OF LOVE
HAS BROKEN MANY A HEART,
DISRUPTED MARRIAGES,
AND WAS KNOWN TO START
A HISTORICAL WAR
IN A ONCE PEACEFUL LAND
BY PROMISING A MORTAL
ANOTHER WOMAN'S HAND.
AS APHRODITE RIDES
IN A CHARIOT DRAWN
BY DOVES
AND SPARROWS
AND ELEGANT SWANS,
MORTALS
IMMORTALS
WARRIORS
AND WISE
MEN LOSE THEIR WITS
WHEN HER ENCHANTING EYES
HYPNOTIZE THEIR *HEARTS*
AND RIPPLE THEIR *SOULS*
WITH WARMTH FROM HER SMILE
GLIMMERING GOLD,
ILLUMINATING HER FORM
FOR ALL EYES TO SEE
THE BREATHTAKING GLORY
OF GODDESS
APHRODITE.

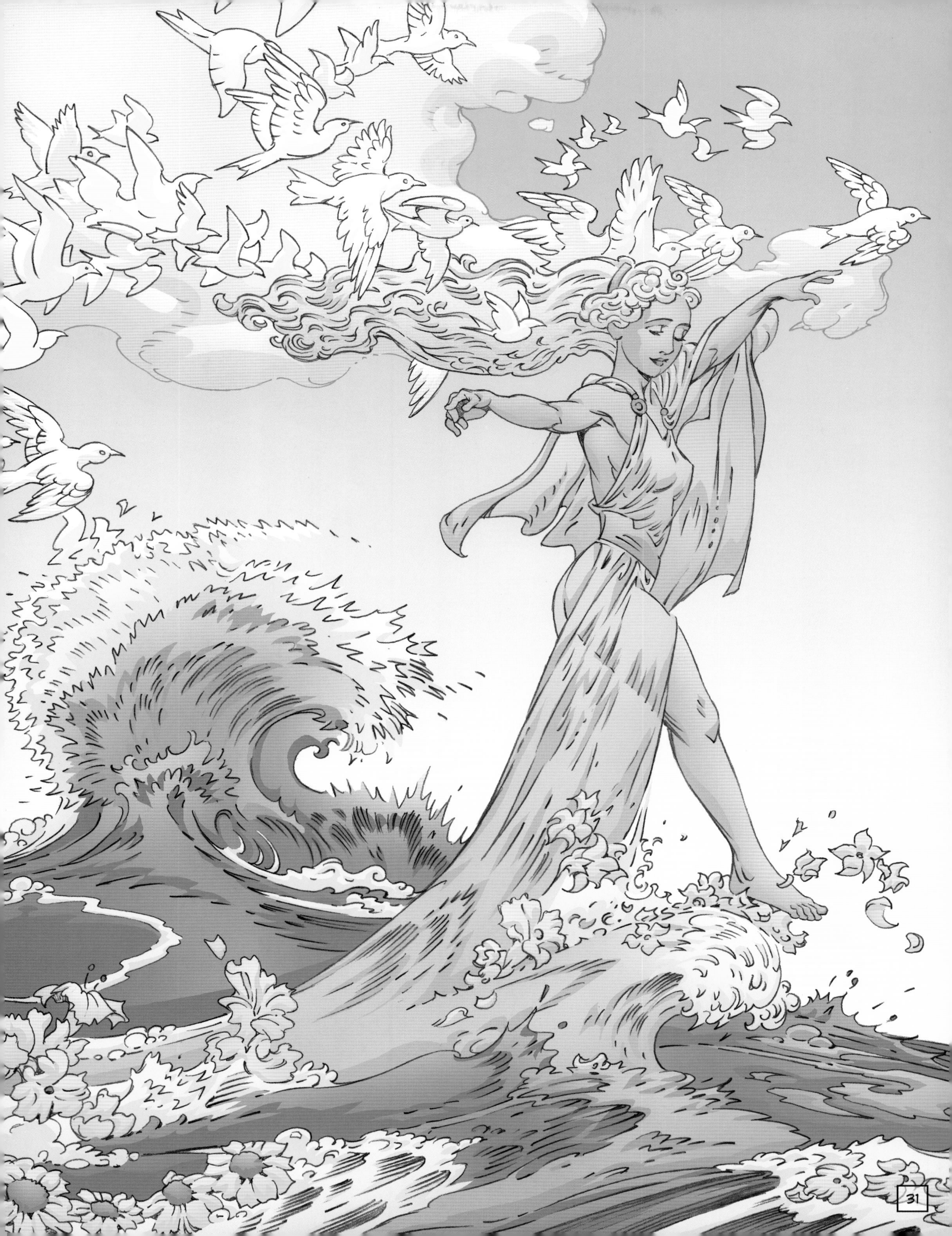

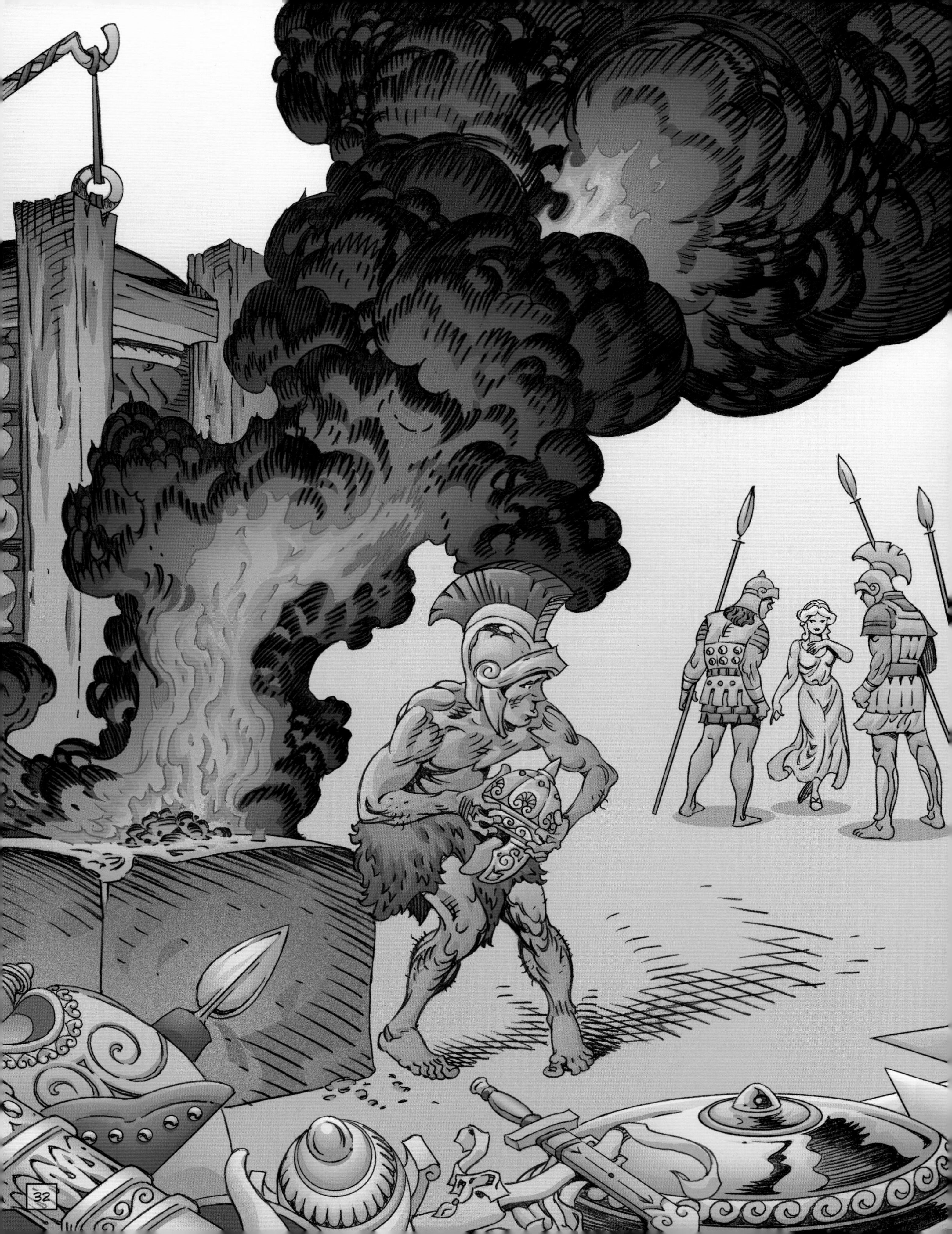

HEPHAESTUS
GOD OF THE FORGE AND FIRE

AMBER SPARKS FLY
WHEN *HEPHAESTUS* WIELDS
HIS WELL-WORN HAMMER
ON HEAT-SOFTENED STEEL,
STRIKING
AND SHAPING
AND HANDCRAFTING METAL
AS GOD OF THE FORGE
SERVING GODS AND MORTALS:
ATHENA'S SHINING SHIELD,
THUNDERBOLTS FOR ZEUS,
HADES' INVISIBLE HELMET,
AND HERMES' MAGIC SHOES.
BUT ON MOUNT OLYMPUS,
OF ALL THE GODS,
ONLY HEPHAESTUS
IS PHYSICALLY FLAWED.
HIS LEGS WERE *DEFORMED*
AND PERMANENTLY BROKEN
WHEN ZEUS OR HERA,
HIS PARENTS, FLUNG HIM
FROM HIGH ON OLYMPUS
WHERE HE FELL FOR NINE DAYS
AND *SMASHED* INTO ROCKS
SURROUNDED BY WAVES.
TO THE SEA HE PLUNGED,
AND THERE HE WAS RAISED
BY THE SEA GODDESS THETIS
IN AN OCEAN CAVE,
WHERE HE HONED THE ART

AND CRAFT OF HIS TRADE,
CREATING TROPICAL FISH
FROM JEWELS THAT HE MADE
TO HONOR HIS NEW
MOTHER BECAUSE SHE
RAISED HIM WITH LOVE
UNCONDITIONALLY.
BUT SINCE HE IS SMALL,
LAME, AND NOT BEAUTIFUL,
ALL THE GODS TREAT
HEPHAESTUS WITH *RIDICULE*;
ESPECIALLY HIS VERY
OWN WIFE, APHRODITE,
WHO CHEATS ON HIM
WITH OTHER MEN CONSTANTLY.
STILL
HIS SKILL
EARNED HIM THE REPUTATION
AS THE ULTIMATE CRAFTSMAN
WHOSE EVERY CREATION
NEVER FAILS TO *AWE*
NEVER FAILS TO *INSPIRE*
WHEN HIS HAMMERING HANDS
SCULPT, WITH FIRE,
METAL INTO ART
THAT ALL ADMIRE
FROM HIS VOLCANIC FORGE
EXHALING HIGH
PLUMES OF SMOKE,
CHOKING THE SKY.

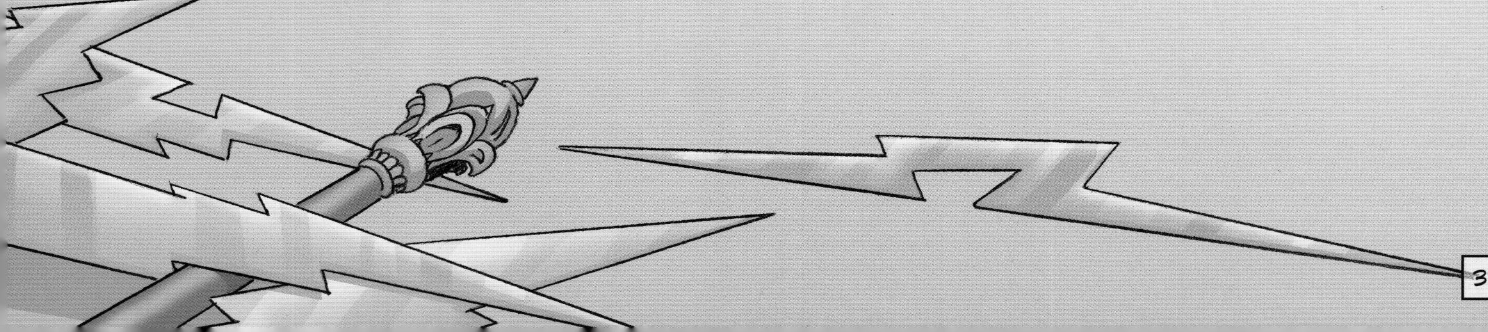

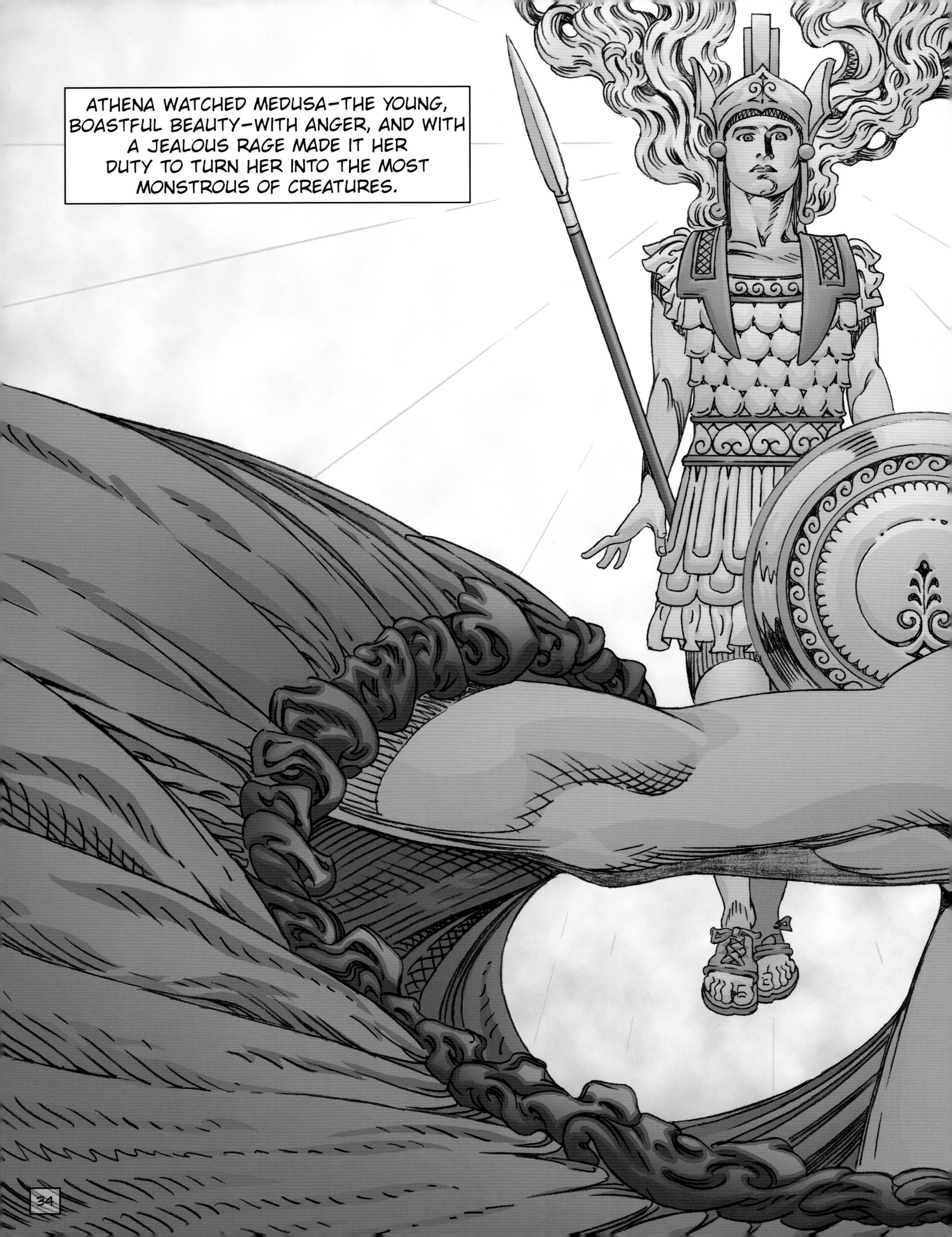
ATHENA WATCHED MEDUSA—THE YOUNG, BOASTFUL BEAUTY—WITH ANGER, AND WITH A JEALOUS RAGE MADE IT HER DUTY TO TURN HER INTO THE MOST MONSTROUS OF CREATURES.

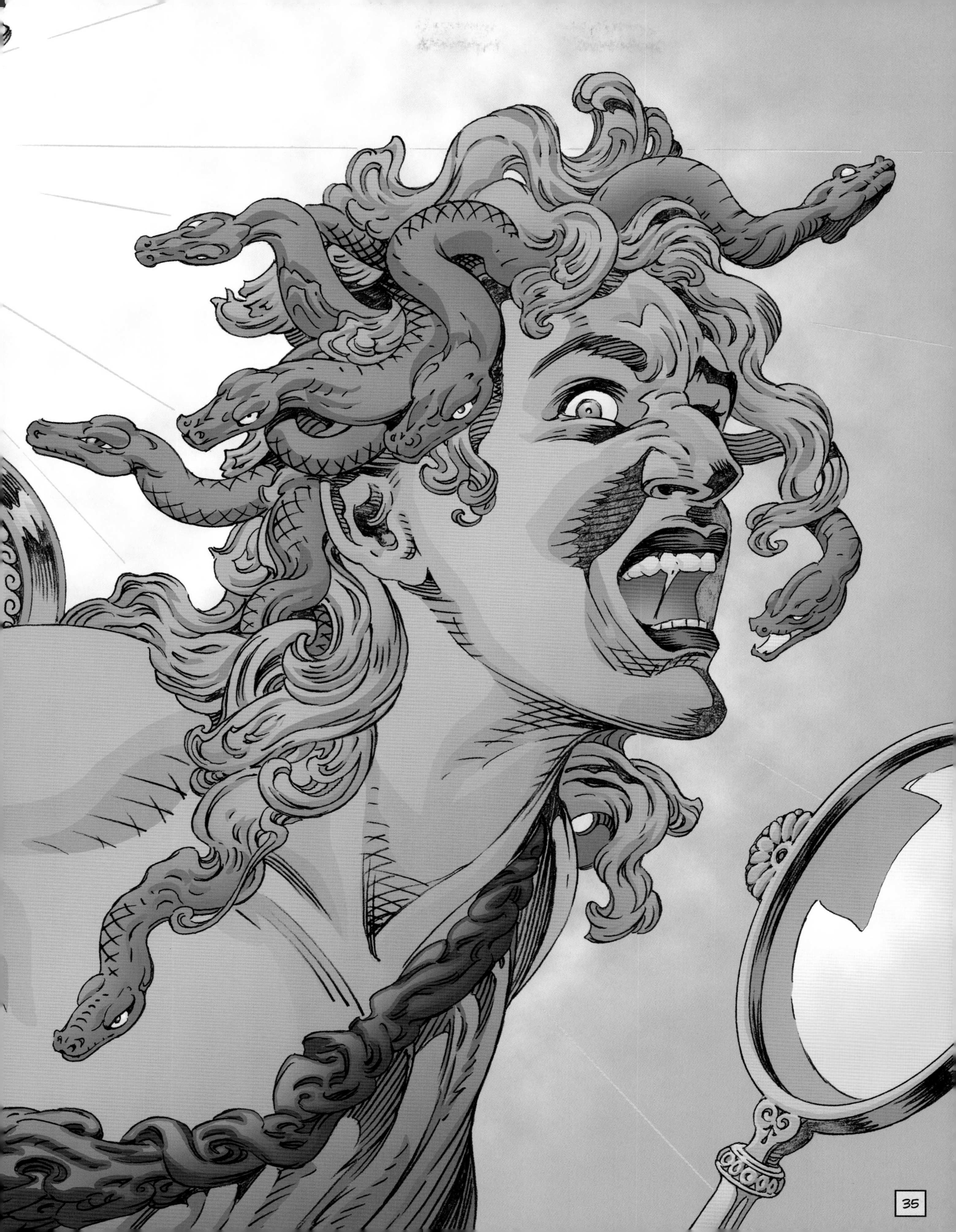

ATHENA GODDESS OF WISDOM

FROM THE SKULL OF ZEUS,
SHRIEKING FIERCE BATTLE CRIES,
SPRANG **ATHENA**, THE GODDESS
OF WISDOM, WITH EYES
FLASHING LIKE LIGHTNING,
WEARING ARMOR OF GOLD
FROM HELMET TO FOOT,
A STUNNING SIGHT TO BEHOLD.
A SHIELD IN HER LEFT HAND
A SPEAR IN HER RIGHT,
THE WARRIOR GODDESS
MIXES **MIND** AND **MIGHT**
ON THE FIELD OF BATTLE
WITH A BRAVE HEART,
BUT OFF THE FIELD
SHE'S THE GODDESS OF ART,
INVENTING THE BRIDLE
FOR MAN TO TAME HORSES,
INVENTING THE SAIL
TO HARNESS GALE FORCES.
BUT HER MOST **GENEROUS**
GIFT WAS A TREE
BEARING OLIVES THAT SHE
GAVE TO A GREEK CITY
THAT HONORED HER
BY TAKING HER NAME—
ATHENS—AND SOON
THE CITY BECAME
RICH THROUGH HER GIFT
AND HOME TO HER TEMPLE,

THE PARTHENON, WHERE MORTALS
WENT SEEKING HER COUNSEL.
GIVING THEIR EAR
TO THE GODDESS OF CLEAR
VISION AND THOUGHT
TO OVERCOME FEAR
IN TIMES OF DESPAIR
OR IN TIMES OF WAR,
HER **WISDOM**-FILLED WORDS
TO MERE MORTALS OR
FUTURE HEROES
HELPS TO SLAY FOES
OF ALL SHAPES AND SIZES
WITH CALCULATED BLOWS.
SURROUNDED BY SOLDIERS
IS WHEN SHE SHINES BEST,
PROTECTED IN ARMOR
COVERING HER CHEST,
STANDING WITH CALM
ON THE BATTLEFIELD,
RAISING HER SPEAR,
CLUTCHING HER SHIELD,
HAMMERED BY HEPHAESTUS
AND SKETCHED WITH THE FACE
OF THE MONSTROUS MEDUSA
CROWNED WITH SNAKES,
ATHENA FLASHES
BOLTS FROM EACH EYE
AND LEADS THE CHARGE
WITH HER **THUNDEROUS** CRY.

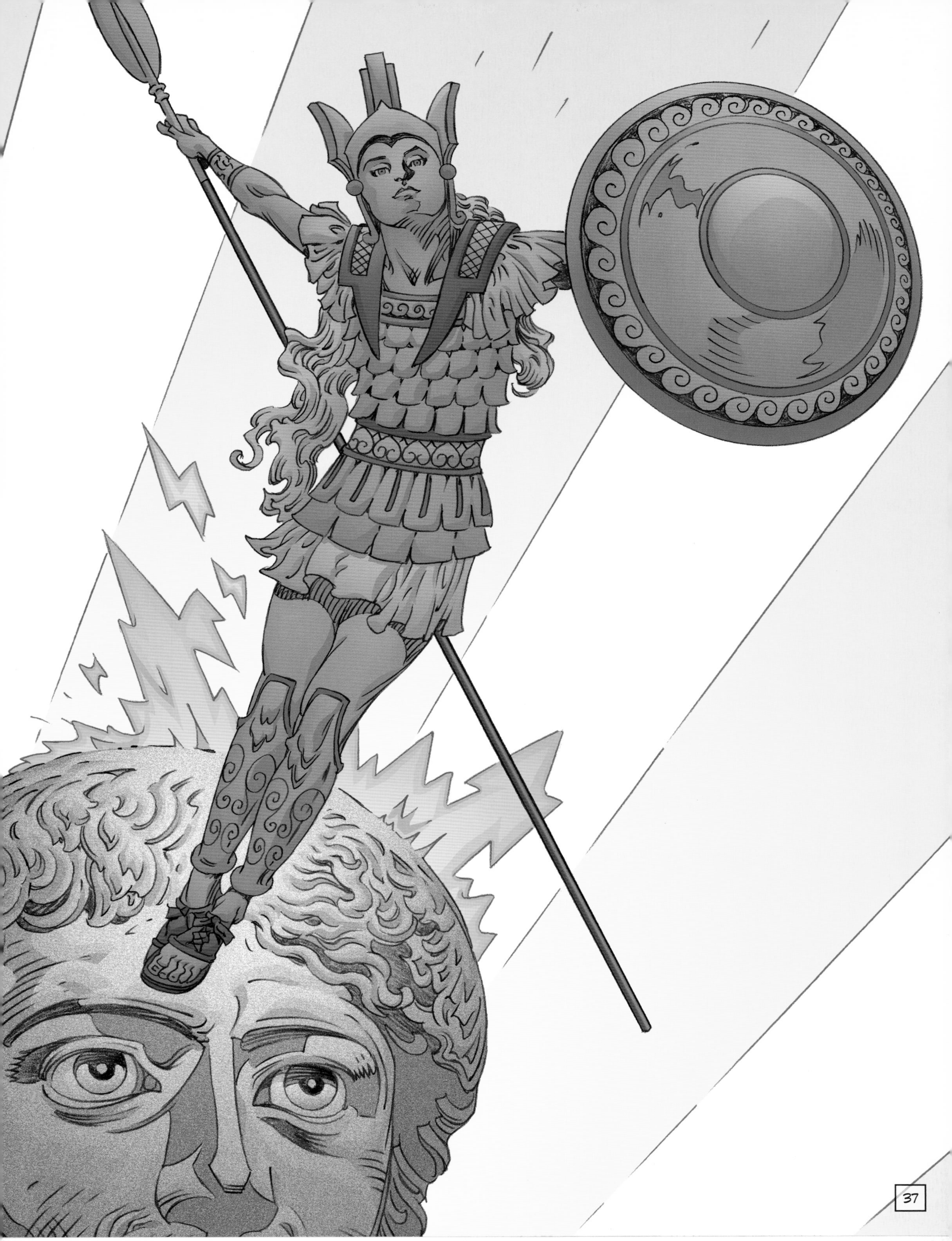

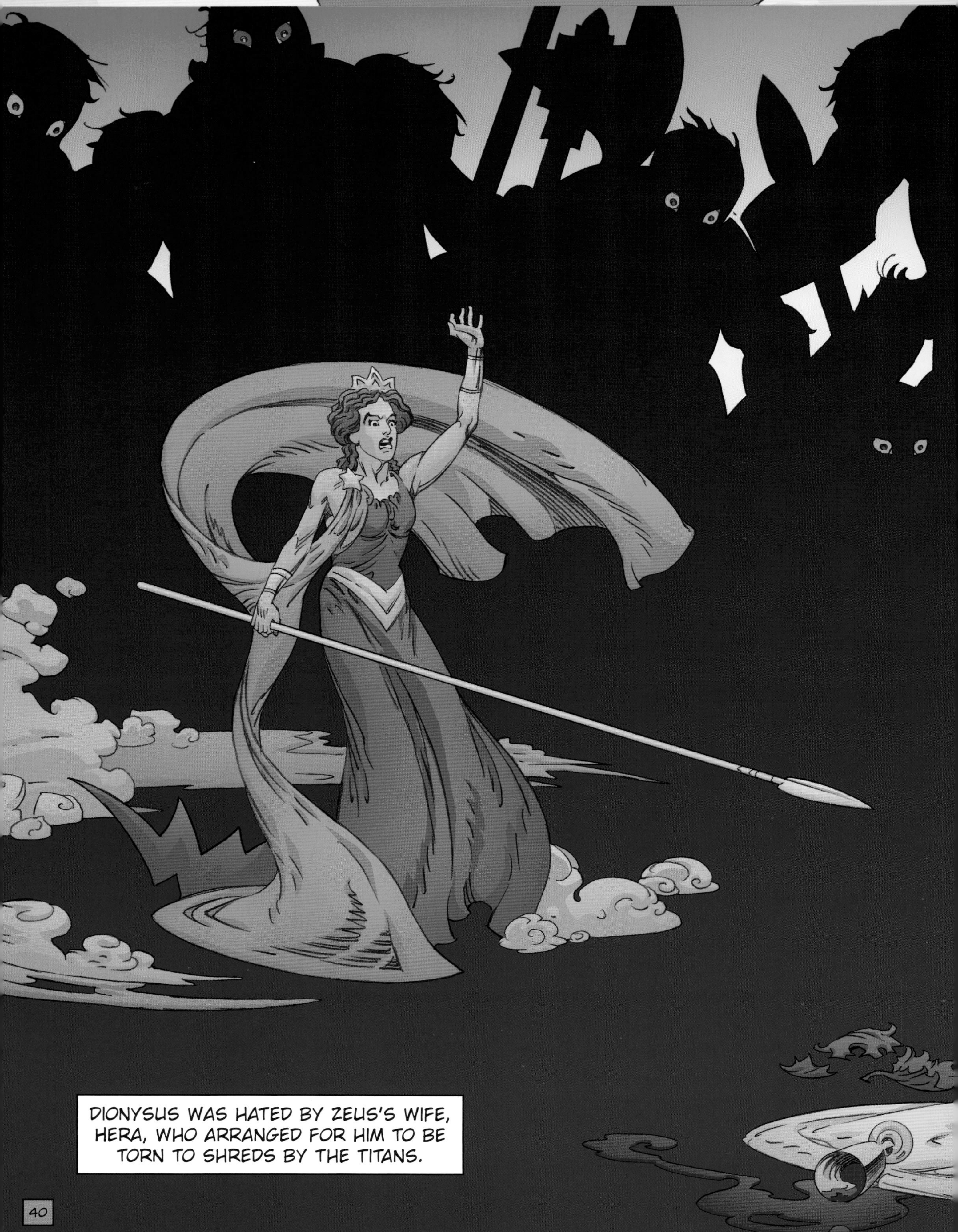
DIONYSUS WAS HATED BY ZEUS'S WIFE, HERA, WHO ARRANGED FOR HIM TO BE TORN TO SHREDS BY THE TITANS.

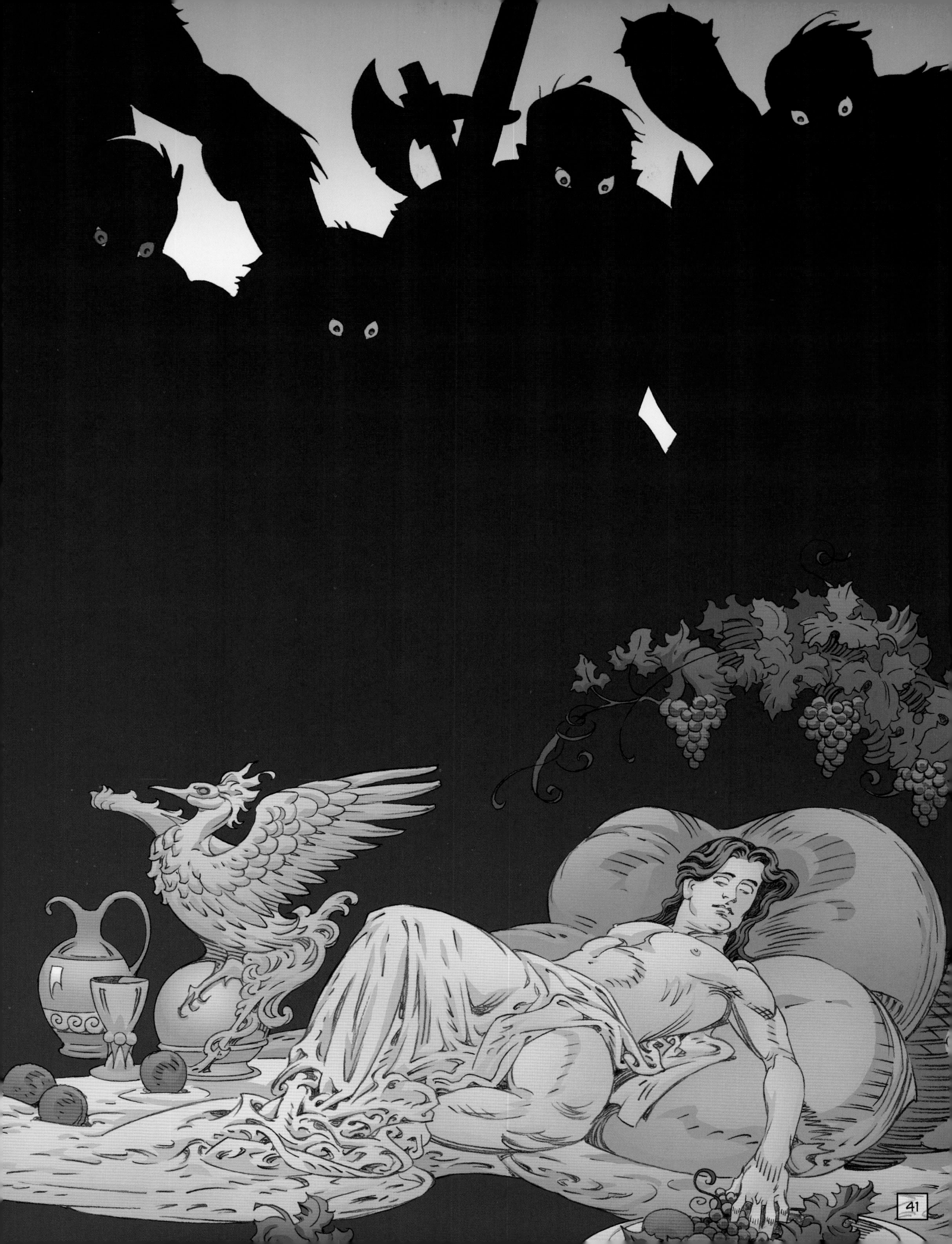

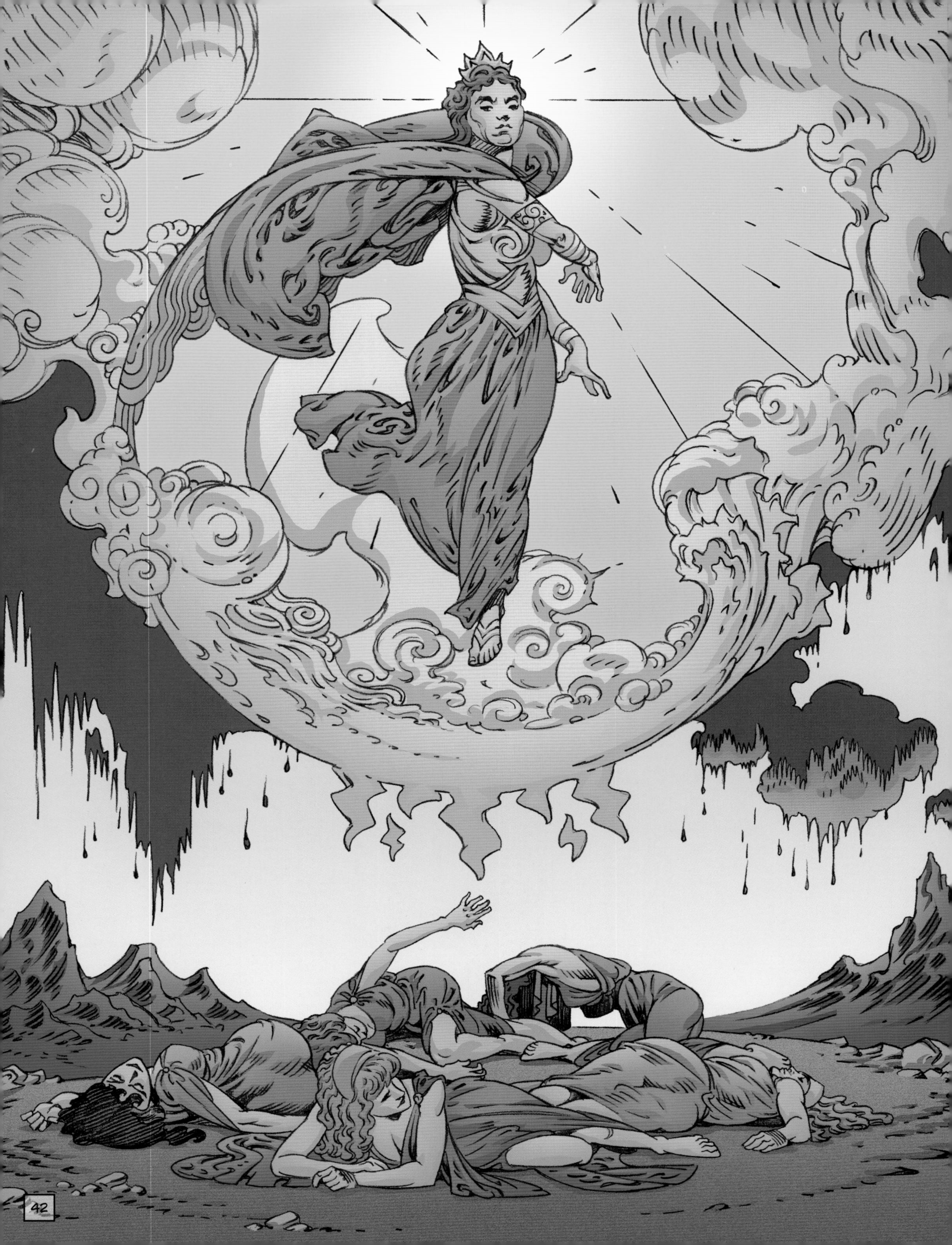

HERA
SUPREME GODDESS, GODDESS OF MARRIAGE

WITH CURLS CRIMSON RED
CASCADING DOWN
HER IMMORTAL HEAD
TOPPED WITH A CROWN,
QUEEN GODDESS *HERA*
SITS PERCHED ON HER THRONE
ATOP MOUNT OLYMPUS
WITH HER PEACOCK'S EYES ON
HER HUSBAND, ZEUS,
WHO SHIFTS HIS SHAPE
AND DISGUISES HIS FORM
TO DECEIVE AND TAKE
ADVANTAGE OF LOVERS,
INFLAMING HIS WIFE,
HERA, THE GODDESS
OF MARRIAGE WHO LIKES,
NO, *LOVES*, TO TAKE
REVENGE ON WOMEN WHO
FALL UNDER THE SPELL
OR BEAR CHILDREN TO ZEUS.
CURSING OR BURNING
ALL ROMANTIC RIVALS,
HERA *PERSISTS*
IN MAKING SURVIVAL
DIFFICULT FOR ALL
WOMEN ZEUS DESIRES;
MORPHING MOTHERS WHO CHEAT
INTO *VAMPIRES*
WITH A SWEET TOOTH
FOR THEIR OWN CHILDREN,
UNVEILING HER VINDICTIVE
SIDE WHEN THREATENED,
SHOWING TO ALL
THAT THE GODDESS SUPREME
CAN BE THE COLDHEARTED
QUEEN
OF MEAN.

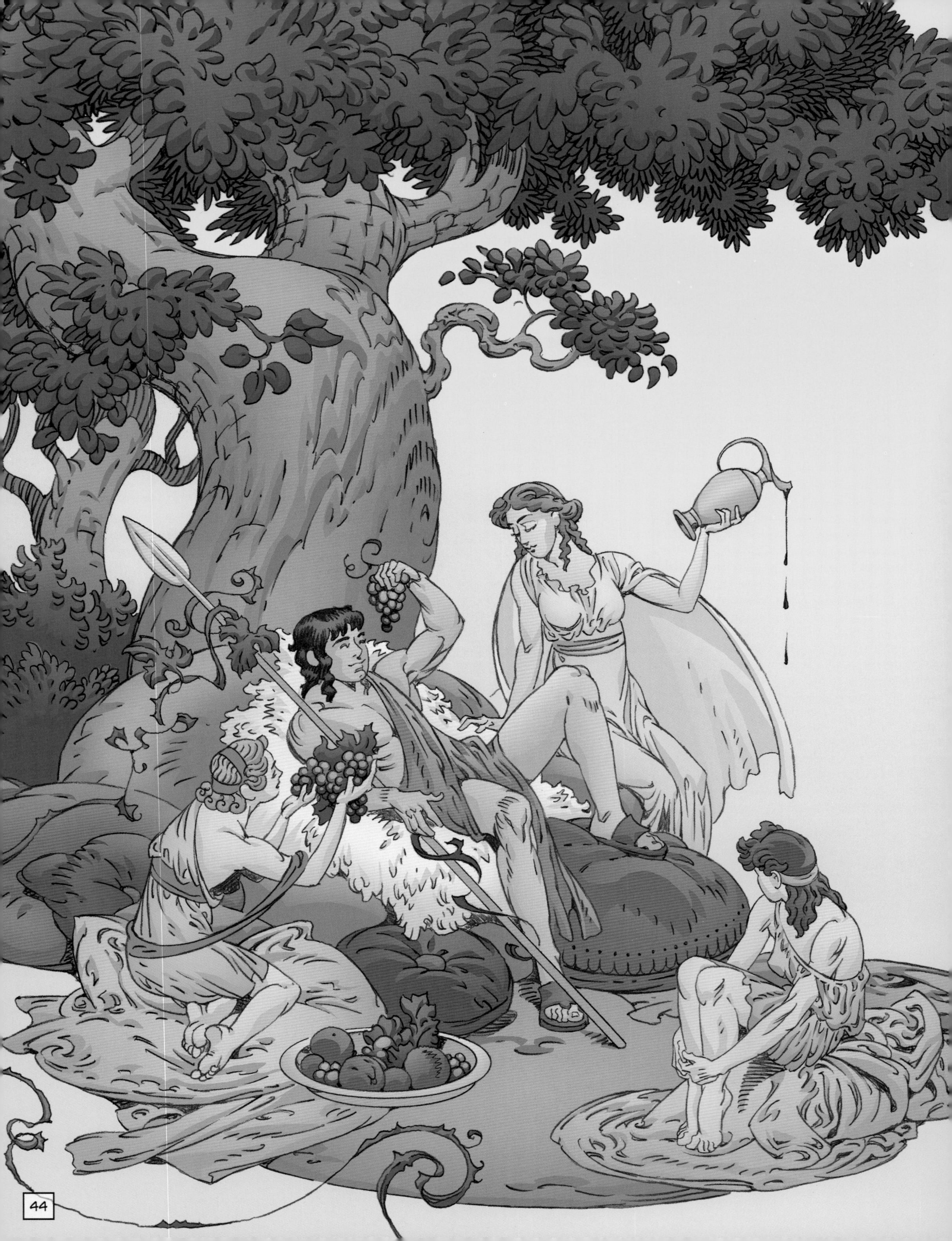

DIONYSUS
GOD OF WINE AND REVELRY

FRESH-FACED AND YOUNG
WITH CURLS WREATHED IN VINES,
DANCES *DIONYSUS*,
GOD OF REVELRY AND WINE,
THE DUAL-NATURED DEITY
WHO TRAVELS THE LAND
SPREADING PLEASURE AND MADNESS
WITH IMMORTAL HANDS.
PLEASURE FROM THE TASTE
OF FERMENTED GRAPES,
MADNESS FROM MERRIMENT
IN A LIBERATED STATE
INDUCED BY THE RESTLESS
GOD OF THE VINE,
WHO SPENDS HIS EXISTENCE
LOOKING FOR A GOOD TIME.
BORN OF ZEUS
AND A MORTAL LOVER,
HE WAS *HATED*
BY ZEUS'S WIFE, HERA,
WHO ARRANGED FOR HIM
TO BE TORN TO SHREDS
BY THE TITANS, BUT ONE OF THEM
BROUGHT HIM BACK FROM THE DEAD.
RISING WITH LIFE
AFTER HEAVING HIS LAST
BREATH FROM HIS CHEST,
HE *AROSE* WITH A GASP
MAKING HIM ONE
OF THE FEW GODS WHO COULD
RETRIEVE A SOUL

FROM THE UNDERWORLD.
RAISED IN THE WOODLANDS
BY NYMPHS, WITH AFFECTION,
HE BECAME KNOWN
AS THE GOD OF RESURRECTION.
LAUGHING THROUGH LIFE
WITH A BRIGHT, EASY SMILE,
DIONYSUS IS KNOWN
TO UNLEASH HIS WILD
SIDE WHEN TESTED,
DOUBTED, OR PROVOKED
USING TENDRILS OF VINES
TO SUFFOCATE AND CHOKE
THE LIFE OUT OF THOSE
WHO INSULT OR CAPTURE
THE MERRYMAKING GOD
WHO FILLS HEARTS WITH RAPTURE.
CLUTCHING A SPEAR
COVERED IN GREEN
IVY AND GRAPEVINES,
SURROUNDED BY MEAN
PAWING PANTHERS
AND TEETH-BARING TIGERS
READY TO POUNCE
WHEN THE YOUNG GOD DESIRES,
DIONYSUS COMMANDS
HIS CATS TO SAVAGERY
WHILE STANDING TALL
AND *LAUGHING*
IN REVELRY.

WHO'S WHO

Why did I choose to call these gods and goddesses "The Mighty Twelve"? First of all, they are officially known as Olympians (because they live on Mount Olympus). Most of them are very well known and have been etched in our memory through references in art, literature, and the English language itself. But most of all, these twelve remind me of superheroes, and sometimes villians, with special powers—who also sometimes have had difficulty fitting in with "regular" people (that is, mortals). They are good, bad, gifted, imperfect—and to me, the most interesting of the gods. Those who have studied mythology might notice that two Olympians are not given specific attention in this book: Persephone, Goddess of the Underworld; and Hestia, Goddess of the Hearth. While their powers do not seem strong enough to merit an entire poem, they are mentioned in the introduction to the book. One Olympian, Dionysus, is often left out because of his birth (his mother is mortal) and his connection to Zeus, but nonetheless he is an Olympian, and after reading his poem you will see he merits just as much attention as the others included. Finally, it should be clear that Cerberus and Medusa are not considered Olympians, nor are they gods, but their connection to the Olympians ties several stories together and helps you, the reader, become immersed in this mythological world.

APHRODITE (AF-RUH-DIE-TEE)**:**
GODDESS OF LOVE AND BEAUTY
Parents: the Titan Uranus, no mother
Symbols: dove, myrtle tree, rose, apple, sparrow, swan
Special Powers/Weapons/Tools: a magical girdle that causes everyone to fall in love with the wearer
Did you know? The Trojan War began because Aphrodite promised the mortal Helen to Paris if he judged Aphrodite the fairest of all goddesses. (See lines 42–46 in the poem on page 30.)

APOLLO (AH-PAH-LO)**:**
GOD OF LIGHT AND MUSIC
Also known as: The Bright One, Lord of the Silver Bow, God of Truth, God of Prophecy, The Mouse God
Parents: Zeus and the Titaness Leto
Symbols: mouse, sun, lyre, raven, laurel, dolphin, crow
Special Powers/Weapons/Tools: bow and arrow, the power to foretell the future
Did you know? At just four days old, Apollo (and his twin, Artemis) killed the monster Python, a giant serpent, with arrows for harassing his mother during her pregnancy.

ARES (AIR-EEZ)**:**
GOD OF WAR AND STRIFE
Parents: Zeus and Hera
Symbols: spear, burning torch, dog, vulture
Special Powers/Weapons/Tools: When joined by his sister and sons on the battlefield, the ground flows with blood.
Did you know? Ares was captured and bound in chains by two giants, Ephialtes and Otus, as a prank. They stuffed him into a bronze jar, where he remained for thirteen months. The mother of the twin giants told Hermes, who rescued Ares.

ARTEMIS (AR-TUH-MISS)**:**
GODDESS OF THE HUNT AND THE MOON
Also known as: The Lady of Wild Things, Moon Goddess, Protectress of Youth
Parents: Zeus and the Titaness Leto
Symbols: cypress tree, all wild animals (especially the deer)
Special Powers/Weapons/Tools: silver bow and arrow
Did you know? She turned a hunter into a deer for unexpectedly spying on her while bathing. His own hounds hunted him to his death. (See lines 41–42 in the poem on page 25.)

ATHENA (AH-THEE-NA)**:**
GODDESS OF WISDOM
Also known as: Goddess of the City, Gray-eyed Athena, Pallas Athene
Parents: Zeus
Symbols: owl, olive
Special Powers/Weapons/Tools: helmet, shield, and armor
Did you know? She and Poseidon fought over who would name what is now Athens. Each of them gave the city a gift. In some stories, Poseidon offered a horse, which was seen as a symbol of war; Athena gave an olive tree, which was viewed as a symbol of peace. (See lines 21–27 in the poem on page 36.)

CERBERUS (SIR-BUH-RUS)**:**
GUARD DOG TO THE UNDERWORLD
(NOT ONE OF THE GODS)
Parents: the monsters Typhon and Echidne

Special Powers/Weapons/Tools: three heads, poisonous saliva

Did you know? When Cerberus dripped saliva onto the ground, it formed into a poisonous flower called an aconite.

DIONYSUS (DIE-OH-NIE-SUS): GOD OF WINE AND REVELRY
Parents: son of Zeus and the mortal Semele
Symbols: grape, rose, ivy, panther, goat, dolphin
Special Powers/Weapons/Tools: a stick entwined with vine leaves; inspires madness
Did you know? Dionysus was once captured by pirates and turned into a slave aboard a ship. As the pirates tried to shackle the god, he turned the waves into wine that crashed over the ship. Vines spread out over the sails. Then he turned all of the sailors into dolphins, except for the one man who believed Dionysus was a god.

HADES (HAY-DEEZ): GOD OF THE UNDERWORLD
Also known as: The Rich One, The God of Wealth
Parents: Cronus and Rhea (Titans)
Symbols: Jewels and minerals
Special Powers/Weapons/Tools: a helmet that makes the wearer invisible
Did you know? The dead were buried with a coin under their tongue to pay for the journey across the River Styx, which was the last stop before the Underworld.

HEPHAESTUS (HEF-EEST-OSS): GOD OF THE FORGE AND FIRE
Parents: Hera and Zeus (although some say just Hera)
Symbols: fire, quail (because it does a limping dance in spring)
Special Powers/Weapons/Tools: hammer and anvil
Did you know? All of the gods' thrones were created and crafted by Hephaestus, his own being the most elaborate, with rare jewels and the ability to move and roll in any direction.

HERA (HAIR-A): SUPREME GODDESS, GODDESS OF MARRIAGE
Parents: Cronus and Rhea (Titans)
Symbols: cow, peacock, pomegranate

Special Powers/Weapons/Tools: able to morph mortals into anything she chooses

Did you know? Hera honored her one-hundred-eyed servant Argus by setting his eyes in the tail of the peacock.

HERMES (HER-MEEZ): MESSENGER OF THE GODS
Also known as: Master Thief, Divine Herald
Parents: Zeus & the Titaness Maia
Symbols: winged hat and sandals; caduceus (kuh-DOO-see-us), a staff with entwined snakes and a pair of wings above
Special Powers/Weapons/Tools: ability to fly between Olympus, Earth, and the Underworld
Did you know? Hermes put his staff between two fighting snakes, forcing them to stop, and they remained forever entwined on his staff.

HESTIA (HESS-TEE-A): GODDESS OF THE HEARTH
Parents: Cronus and Rhea (Titans)
Symbols: hearth fire
Did you know? While Hestia has no special powers or attributes, she was worshiped all across Greece wherever there was a household cooking fire. She never left Olympus, but she was admired and loved everywhere.

MEDUSA (MI-DOO-SA): GORGON
(NOT ONE OF THE GODDESSES)
Parents: Phorcys (FOR-sis), a sea god; and Ceto, a sea monster
Symbols: snake
Special Powers/Weapons/Tools: turns anyone who looks at her into stone
Did you know? When Medusa's head was cut off, the winged horse Pegasus and a warrior named Chrysaor (KRIS-or) sprang out of her still-bleeding neck.

PERSEPHONE (PER-SE-FUH-NEE): GODDESS OF THE UNDERWORLD
Parents: Zeus and Demeter
Symbols: pomegranate
Did you know? When Hades kidnapped Persephone to be his wife, her mother, Demeter, the Goddess of the Earth and Harvest, became so sad that she neglected the earth and it became barren. When Persephone was found, Zeus told her that she had to spend three months of the year in the Underworld because she had eaten food there. Her mother spends this time

mourning her during these months when nothing grows and the earth remains barren. We know this time of the year as winter.

POSEIDON (PUH-SEYE-DUN): **GOD OF THE SEA**
Also known as: Earth-shaker
Parents: Cronus and Rhea (Titans)
Symbols: trident, horse
Special Powers/Weapons/Tools: controls waves, causes earthquakes
Did you know? Poseidon created the first horse, inspired by the shape of a curling wave.

TITANS (TIE-TANS): **THE ELDER GODS**
Names: Cronus, Rhea, Ocean, Leto, Tethys, Hyperion, Mnemosyne (NEE-MOS-AH-NEE), Themis, Iapetus, Coeus, Phoebe, Theia, Crius
Family Status: the generation of gods and goddesses prior to the Olympians
Special Features: enormous size, incredible strength
Did you know? When the two Titans Cronus and Rhea had children, it was foretold that one of Cronus's children would try to overthrow him for control of the universe. He decided to take matters into his own hands

and swallowed all six of them (Hestia, Demeter, Hera, Hades, Poseidon, and Zeus) before that could happen. Or so he thought. His wife, Rhea, managed to save their sixth child, Zeus, by hiding his body and replacing it with a large stone that she fed to her husband. Years later, Zeus freed his brothers and sisters by forcing Cronus to vomit them. The siblings then waged a battle for supremacy of the universe against all of the Titans, which lasted ten years. Once beaten, the Titans were driven beneath the earth and locked up in chains.

ZEUS (ZOOS): **KING OF THE GODS**
Also known as: Lord of the Bright Sky, Lord of the Dark Storm Cloud, The Cloud Gatherer
Parents: Cronus and Rhea (Titans)
Symbols: eagle, scepter, oak tree, thunderbolt
Special Powers/Weapons/Tools: thunderbolt; controls clouds; has ability to morph himself, as well as mortals, as he chooses
Did you know? Zeus pursued the hand of Hera for 300 years. Eventually he turned himself into a dove that appeared half-frozen from the rain. Hera took pity on the bird and cared for it, and Zeus revealed himself and she fell in love.

BIBLIOGRAPHY

Any book on mythology is bound to be shaped by different variations of the stories, and this one is no exception. Legend grows out of the ancient oral traditions of performing epic poetry, song, and storytelling, and is passed on from generation to generation. Even after some were written down, many versions developed over the years. For the purposes of this book I referred to a number of sources and reviewed certain stories against others to seek the most consistent "facts" about the gods and goddesses. Nonetheless there are still stories that might appear one place and not another. If you'd like to read more about the Greek gods and goddesses, you can check out these great books that I used as part of my research for this book:

Allan, Tony. *Titans and Olympians: Greek and Roman Myth (Myth and Mankind)*. Lanham, MD: Barnes and Noble Books, 2003.

D'Aulaire, Ingri and Edgar. *D'Aulaire's Book of Greek Myths*. New York: Bantam Dell. Originally published 1962.

Evans, Cheryl, Anne Millard, and Rodney Matthews. *The Usborne Book of Greek and Norse Legends*. Tulsa: EDC Publishing, 1987.

Evslin, Bernard. *Cerberus (Monsters of Mythology series)*. New York: Chelsea House, 1987.

Evslin, Bernard. *Medusa (Monsters of Mythology series)*. New York: Chelsea House, 1987.

Evslin, Bernard. *Heroes, Gods and Monsters of the Greek Myths*. New York: Laurel-Leaf Books, 1984.

Graves, Robert. *Greek Gods and Heroes*. New York: Laurel-Leaf Books. Originally published 1965.

Hamilton, Edith. *Mythology*. New York: Warner Books, 1998.

McCaughrean, Geraldine and Emma Chichester Clark. *Greek Gods and Goddesses*. New York: Margaret K. McElderry Books, 1998.

Hathaway, Nancy. *The Friendly Guide to Mythology*. New York: Penguin Books, 2001.

Homer. *The Iliad*.

Homer. *The Odyssey*.

Petras, Kathryn. Fandex Family Field Guides. *Mythology*. New York: Workman Publishing, 1998.